"Holly,

"I love you, too. I'll be interested in hearing you later when you are feeling better."

"Promise?" Holly's smile in return touched his heart.

"I promise, Bryce. Remember the night in the barn when I wanted to kiss you?"

He nodded.

"You said you would wait until I knew for certain what kind of love I have for you. I know now. So now I am asking you to wait until you are fully recovered. You said you wanted it to be special, and I do, too."

He released her. "Absolutely. Until then I shall continue to dream."

Holly giggled. "And so will I."

Bryce groaned. "You are sure you want to wait? I wouldn't mind kissing you right now."

"But I would!" John Graham's harsh voice boomed throughout the room.

LYNN A. COLEMAN

is an award-winning and bestselling author and the founder of American Christian Fiction Writers organization. She writes fiction full-time and loves visiting places like Savannah and other historical locations. She makes her home in Florida with her husband of thirty-nine years. Together they are blessed with three children and eight grandchildren.

LYNN A. COLEMAN

Courting Holly

HEARTSONG
PRESENTS

Recycling programs
for this product may
not exist in your area.

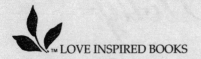

™ LOVE INSPIRED BOOKS

ISBN-13: 978-0-373-48673-1

COURTING HOLLY

Copyright © 2013 by Lynn A. Coleman

www.LoveInspiredBooks.com

Printed in U.S.A.

Trust in the LORD with all thine heart; and lean not unto thine own understanding. In all thy ways acknowledge him, and he shall direct thy paths.
—*Proverbs* 3:5–6

I'd like to dedicate this book to Eleanor Debaucher. Officially, she is my husband's aunt, but her love and kindness is so sweet that I've adopted her as my aunt, as well. Thank you for all the many times you let me crash at your place while I was working on research for this story. All my love.

Chapter 1

Holly gripped her mother's hand. The licorice-like scent of laudanum assaulted her nostrils. How could something to ease terrible pain smell so sweet? "Momma…"

"Holly, in my Bible…" Her mother's chest rose with a great deal of effort then fell. "There's a letter." Another labored breath. "Explains all…" She paused. "Forgive me." Momma's deep green eyes darkened.

"Momma, there is nothing to forgive." Holly grasped her mother's hand tighter. Her own breathing labored as she eased closer to her mother on the bed.

"Your father…" The words were raspier.

"He's right here, Momma."

"No, real father…" Holly looked over at her father. His dark brown eyes pierced hers and his lips parted. His drawn features flickered with the glow from the oil lamp.

"Emmett Landers…schoolteacher…" Holly's gaze returned to her mother.

"Allison," her father interrupted, "I'll tell her. You relax."

Real father? Momma must be delusional from all the laudanum and other pain medications. All Holly's life she'd lived in this house on the Savannah coast. Her father was always there. From the earliest of her memories he'd been at her side encouraging her, loving her. Mother must be confused.

Father caressed her mother's forehead, brushing away the red strands, and kissed her gently.

"Forgive me, Holly. Forgive me." Her eyes were wide with fear.

"I forgive you, Momma." What else could she say? She'd been called to her mother's room, having spent the past hours in the kitchen taking care of Momma's chores. Tiffany, her sister, was old enough to help, and she'd done some of the work, but Holly wanted her to continue with her studies.

Father nodded and Mother's eyelids closed. Her lips moved. No discernible words passed through. Holly's stomach twisted. Tears burned the edges of her eyes. Momma was dying and there wasn't anything anyone could do. *God, where are you? Why are you letting this happen to such a good woman?*

Bryce paced outside the Grahams' bedroom door and wrung his hat. It wasn't right that someone as kind and loving as Mrs. Graham—a woman he'd known and admired his entire life—would have been run over by a careless wagon driver. The creak of the door captured his attention. He watched Holly step backward out of the room, her red ponytail draped between her slumped shoulders. She paused and braced herself against the doorjamb. He closed the distance between them. She turned. He wrapped her in his embrace. "I am here, Holly." Her swollen emerald eyes glanced up into his. Her delicate porcelain skin flushed with emotion. He escorted her to the parlor.

"She's dying, Bryce."

"I know."

She burrowed her gaze upon his and knitted her eyebrows. Holly nodded and closed her eyes. A fresh flood of tears ran down her cheeks. "I don't understand why."

"Nor do I." He brushed a strand of her fiery red hair behind her ear. His fingers tingled. This was the closest he'd been to her in years...except in his dreams. He'd been waiting two years for her twenty-first birthday to court her, per her father's request.

Her brilliant green eyes sparkled from tears. "Momma's dying and, and..."

"Shh, you don't need to say a thing, Holly." He pulled her into his arms as they sat on the settee. He didn't care if it was proper or not. She was hurting—and she was his best friend. Maybe more, someday.

While Holly was closer to his sister Catherine's age, it had always been he and Holly who would run off on adventures, read the same stories, engage in long conversations and dream with one another. Only after he'd left for college had he realized his love for Holly was more than that of an unofficial big brother.

She placed her hand on his chest and pushed back. "I am frightened. Momma said..."

He could sense the fear, as if her life were crumbling. "Whatever it is can wait, Holly. Let me give you my strength to help you through this." She eased back into his embrace and placed her head on his shoulder. He resisted opening his heart to her, as he had resisted for the past two years.

He glanced around the room, so familiar. His gaze settled on the leg of the table that had a notch in it. A notch he and Holly were responsible for. His backside and hers had smarted for quite a while after Mrs. Graham caught them playing with their wooden swords as French musketeers in the formal sitting room. The notch in the table leg was nothing compared to the rare handblown glass vase they had knocked over during their battle.

"I brought a pot of Mother's venison stew. I see you have already started some chicken and dumplings."

She nodded.

"Mother said she would visit tomorrow and lend a hand around the house. I will take care of the chores in the barn. Is there anything else I can do?"

"No." She tossed her head from side to side. She pushed away from his shoulder and wiped her eyes with the backs of her hands.

He pulled out a clean white handkerchief. "Here."

She accepted the cloth and dabbed her sparkling green eyes. "I should get back to the kitchen before the dinner burns."

"As you wish. You are certain there is nothing else I can do for you?"

She smiled. "No, not yet. I may need my best friend, though."

"Anytime, any place. You know how to get in touch with me." He leaned over and kissed the top of her head, as he had done when they were mere children. "I will return before I leave."

"Thank you."

"'Tis my pleasure, my lady." He stood and bowed with

the flair of a French musketeer. "I am and always will be your servant." He took her hand and helped her to her feet.

Holly laughed. "I seem to remember quite a few games where you were in charge."

"But of course, I am the oldest." He chuckled.

Holly rolled her eyes heavenward.

It was good to see her smile, even for a moment. "Alas, I must excuse myself and be off to ye ole barn."

"And I to slave over the stove."

Holly stepped into the kitchen, removed the cast-iron pot from the stove and went over to the sink. She glanced out the window and followed Bryce as he meandered down the worn path toward the barn. An unexpected sigh escaped her lips. He carried his muscular six-foot frame with a gentle ease. He turned, saw her in the window and waved. She waved back self-consciously and looked away—but just for a second. A girl could get lost in his honey-brown eyes. Her fingers twitched at the thought of running them through his wavy brown hair. If only...

She shifted her gaze and went back to work.

She stirred the contents of the pot, checked the coals and added several. She cleaned her hands then pulled out the rising dough from the sidewall cabinet of the stove and punched down the swollen batch. The dough should yield three large loaves, or four dozen rolls for the funeral.

The funeral... Dear God, was all hope lost?

Holly pulled and slammed the dough on the floured table. She didn't want her mother to die. She'd spent last night in tears after the doctor told them nothing could be done after the accident. She had snuggled into a fetal position under the covers.

But today was different. Father needed her to be strong, and the entire family depended on her. She slapped the

dough down once again. Mother counted on her to help
with the children. Perhaps that was why she hadn't yet
married, even as she approached the age of twenty-one.
Holly punched the center of the dough. After her mother
was gone, she would be needed to raise her sister and
brothers.

"Holly, may I have a word with you?" Father stood in
the kitchen doorway, interrupting Holly's thoughts. In his
hand he held Momma's Bible.

"Give me a moment to roll out these loaves." Anything
to put off the knowledge she feared.

"Tiffany can finish the bread." He called her sister and
gave his orders, then shifted his gaze back to Holly. With
a lift of his head, he said, "Follow me, please."

"Yes, sir." She loved her father. He was a stern man,
very disciplined, most unlike her. Holly found giggles and
folly in most of life's circumstances. Father enjoyed a laugh
or two every now and again but preferred to keep somber
moments somber. Holly's giddy behavior was in direct con-
trast, and something she had in common with her mother.
They'd agreed years ago it had to be the fire in their hair
that set their blood to easy excitement.

He sat in the leather chair in front of his mahogany desk.
The den was the place where quiet and decorum were kept
at all times. One could play a game of chess, read a book,
speak softly and enjoy sketching or some such sport.

He motioned for her to join him in the matching chair
beside his. "Please take a seat, child."

Holly's knees wobbled. In that moment she knew the
bizarre words her mother had said moments ago were true.
The man beside her was not her father. But how? Why?
What happened? A sinking feeling began in the pit of her
stomach. Was she the product of a violent act done on her
mother? She squeezed her eyes shut. *Please God, no.*

"Holly, I know what your mother said is disconcerting, but relax your fiery imagination for a moment. I will tell you what you need to know." He paused.

"Your mother was married to another before we met. She lived with him on the frontier—for a while. His name was Emmett Landers. He forced your mother to return to Savannah, to your grandparents, with the capable help of an old friend. All of you made it back to Savannah just before the war hit. Your father stayed behind to protect his land and honor. Your mother never heard from him again, until she received word a year later that Emmett had died in battle.

"About that time, you and your mother had caught my attention. I courted your mother for a year and a half before she agreed to marry me. We were married on Christmas day in 1864. You were four at the time. I loved you as if you were my own. You must know that."

Unable to speak, Holly nodded.

"Your father arrived back in Savannah the following year. He hadn't died. Records weren't always accurate. He found out that your mother had remarried and was expecting Tiffany." Her father paused again, more emotional than Holly had ever seen him. "Your mother still loved your father. But she loved me, too. It was a very difficult time for everyone.

"Inside the Bible are three letters. Two are from your father Emmett, one to your mother and one to you. Your letter has not been opened. Your mother wrote a letter to you, as well. I know the contents of Emmett's letter to your mother and your mother's letter to you, but not your letter from your…real father."

He went on, his voice strained. "If you have any questions, I will try my best to answer them. I will admit I am concerned about the contents of Emmett's letter to you. It would be impossible not to be. But you know I am a rational man, Holly, and my concern is not rational. Concern never is, when it comes to a father and his daughters. I am and always will be your father, and my goal is to protect you from harm. However, we agreed to give you these letters on your twenty-first birthday or just before your wedding day. None of us could have foreseen the accident..." his voice faltered "...changing that timetable."

He stood and handed her the Bible. "I'll leave you and close the door behind me. I cannot imagine what kinds of thoughts you are formulating in your mind right now, but you need time to absorb this information." He kissed the top of her head and left the room.

Holly's fingers caressed the well-worn leather, her mind reeling. She'd seen this Bible on her mother's nightstand for years. But it wasn't the one she read on a daily basis. Holly traced the cracked leather on the edges that embraced the pages within. She opened the Bible and found the three letters inside the front cover. The paper was yellow with age and dry. Her mother's script was evident; her father's unknown, but masculine and elegant. Her father was an educated man. Momma said he was a teacher.

She decided to open her mother's letter first.

My dearest daughter,

On March 18, 1861, your father Emmett Landers packed a wagon for you and me to return to Savannah. He had some business that had gone very wrong and feared for our safety. With a great deal of reluctance, and a fair amount of arguing, of which you and I are quite capable, I finally agreed to go. His utmost concern was our safety, and what convinced me to leave him behind was our concern for you.

You are a grown woman now, and I hope you will

understand my keeping your father a secret from you. Your grandparents were not fond of him, and they were pleased with John Graham, your other father. Darling, please understand, Emmett did nothing wrong, apart from taking their beloved daughter out to the Wild West. For this they never forgave him. And when he returned, they were not happy.

I loved your father Emmett with all my heart. Never forget that. I also love John. We have made a good home for ourselves, and a good family. Emmett saw that we were in love, and he also saw how much you loved John. He didn't want to upset you and your life. He had our marriage annulled, allowing John and me to stay together.

My dear daughter, you are probably wondering what was whirling through my head. Why didn't I simply choose one man over the other? Honestly, I couldn't choose at the time. I loved both. But Emmett had been gone from my life for nearly four years by the time I saw him again. I thought I was seeing a ghost. I fainted. Emmett and I spoke briefly, then he left. A week later he returned with the letters and a copy of the annulment. He said his prayer was for our happiness and if we ever needed him, he would come. He agreed to have you wait until your marriage or your twenty-first year before giving you his letter.

I know this is very confusing, and I am sorry. We did what we felt was best at the time. Only you can decide whether we did right by you or not. Forgive me for not having the courage to trust you with this knowledge while you were young. I see a bit of myself in you, as you and I have discussed on several occasions. I know that with my temper, if I were angry enough and had another father, I would have found myself on a train out to Emmett's home in Tennessee. I pray you do not do that in anger. If you wish to visit Emmett, I have a savings in the red purse with the white and purple flowers embroidered on it. You will find the purse in my closet, if I am unable to give it to you at the time.

Love is fragile. Hard work and constant attention are needed to keep the flames of love alive. You will know and understand this after you marry. Emmett was the love of a young girl's heart. We were young and foolish enough to believe we could do anything, go anywhere and survive anything. Unfortunately, we didn't. My love for John took longer to grow, but it is still as deep as with Emmett. The big difference was that I knew love and life could end at any given moment.

When I received word of Emmett's death, a part of me died that day. I think that is what Emmett saw when he came back after the war. I was not the same woman. He also saw my love for John, and John's love for you and me. John is a good man and has guarded our secret.

Forgive me, Holly. I did what I felt was best. I only hope it was the right decision.
Love forever,
Momma

Holly wiped the tears away. Her hands shook. A knock on the door gave her pause. She stood. The door opened. "Holly, forgive me for intruding but…" He cleared his throat. "Your momma has gone home to Jesus."

Her legs turned to mush and she fell to the floor. The letter crumpled in her hand. John Graham swooped her into his arms and sat with her on his lap. They wept together; Holly yielding to great sobs of anguish. Holly loved this man with all her heart. How could he not be her father?

Chapter 2

"Bryce, would you come in here for a moment?"

"Yes, sir." Bryce tapped his soiled boots on the floor mat. Caring for the animals wasn't his normal routine in the morning, but with the foreman ill, someone needed to tend to them.

He entered the den, where his father waited near one of two wing-backed, black-leather chairs, separated by a small table. At the end of the room sat his father's five-foot-long mahogany desk. Bryce's own smaller desk, a mahogany secretary, along with a couple of lamps and bookcases along the walls, took up the rest of the room. Sunlight filtered softly through the tall, lace-covered windows, giving a pleasant warmth to the papered walls. "What can I do for you?" Bryce asked.

"Have a seat, please." His father glanced at his son's attire. Bryce had gone to college to prepare for law, but discovered he preferred business and running the plantation. His father's vision of Bryce as a genteel gentleman lawyer would never come true, and he knew that was a disappointment.

"Sorry for the soiled clothes. The foreman is down with the fever."

His father straightened to his full six feet two inches. "As you know, Allison Graham passed away yesterday."

Bryce nodded. The sting of the news still soured his stomach. The memory of the pain in Holly's eyes made him want to be a constant presence. Apart from a few stolen moments of offering a smile, there had been no opportunity to console.

"There is a history that I am not at liberty to tell you. Client-attorney confidential information."

Bryce nodded for the second time.

"All I can say at this point is that you might need to escort Holly to Tennessee. I would like you to arrange your schedule to be overseen by another for three months. Can you do this for Holly?"

Bryce opened his mouth to speak then closed it shut. What could he say? He understood the confidentiality issue. But why would Holly be involved? And why Tennessee?

He focused on his soiled boots. His mind wandered in a hundred directions. He'd do anything for Holly. He glanced up at his father. "Yes, sir. Whatever is needed." He paused and stood. "Well, forgive me, Father, but if I need to be ready to relinquish my obligations, I must get started. The funeral is in three hours and we will be with the Grahams the rest of the day."

Lloyd squeezed his eyes closed for a moment. "Yes, we shall be very busy. Inform your brothers to be ready to assist the family and escort the children from the graveside."

"Yes, sir. I will take my place beside Holly."

"Thank you. Your mother and I will be helping John with his guests."

"I am angry with Whit Butterfield. How could he be so careless with his carriage? Now a woman is dead."

Lloyd stood and placed a hand on Bryce's shoulder. "It is not our place to judge. I am fighting my own anger, but the Lord reminds me I am not free from sin, either."

"Nor am I," Bryce admitted.

"I am certain Mr. Butterfield is going through his own kind of torment, knowing that his reckless behavior cost a woman her life."

Bryce groaned.

"The day is rapidly getting away from us." Lloyd engaged Bryce in a bear hug and slapped him on the back. "Thank you, son."

"You are welcome, sir," Bryce choked out.

Holly focused on her black-gloved, interlocked fingers. The words her dying mother had shared moments before she'd passed distracted her from the minister's graveside homily more than the sting of the loss.

Long sweeping gowns of Spanish moss draped from the oak trees that lined the main dirt road of the Evergreen Cemetery. Monuments and gravestones dotted the right and left boundaries of the road. Rows of family plots stretched away beneath the arched canopy of ancient trees, each laid out with whatever type of fencing the family wished. The area for her mother's final resting place lay next to her mother's grandparents.

Holly stared at the granite headstone beside the hole where her mother's coffin rested. Its simple engraving pierced her heart. It read, "Emmett Landers Beloved Husband and Father." *Slow, shallow breaths. One. Ease it out slowly. Two.* Holly closed her eyes. A tear fell and slid down her cheek.

The strong hands of Bryce Jarvis embraced the top of her shoulders. Warmth radiated from the palms of his hands down to the bottom of her feet. She'd been longing for his comfort since hearing the truth from her mother. She had almost told him, but what could she have said at that point? Bryce was her best friend and confidant. They had practically grown up together. At one point in her life she had even fancied him and wanted to be his wife. But after he'd returned from college she'd hardly seen him. They would take an occasional walk in the garden after the families shared a meal together. Still, she cherished their ability to talk with one another with ease, something she never experienced with another.

And he was undeniably handsome. Holly smiled, remembering the attractive appearance he made in his top hat and tails as he'd walked toward her before the service began. Then she shook her mind from such foolish thoughts. She was here to bury her mother. She attempted to concentrate on the minister's words.

"Amen," he proclaimed.

"Amen," the graveside crowd replied.

"Allison Graham's family would like to invite all of you back to their home to share some food and fellowship." The new preacher at First Church smiled and tipped the brim of his hat toward Holly and the family.

Bryce leaned in closer. "My family will take care of hosting the meal."

"Thank you." He had no idea how much his love and support meant to her. "Bryce, when you have a minute, could we talk?"

"Whenever you need me, I am here, Holly."

"Thank you."

He held out his elbow. She found herself fitting comfortably in the bend of his strength. He escorted her to the coffin and placed a rose on top. Holly followed suit. "Goodbye, dear one." Bryce's voice strained.

"Goodbye, Momma." She glanced at the nearby stone. "I forgive you," she whispered, but not quiet enough. Bryce heard. He cupped his hand over hers and led her back to the carriage. He didn't ask, and she didn't offer. Soon she would tell her best friend the truth.

She glanced back at Emmett's tombstone… *Why?*

Tiffany and her brothers followed, each escorted by a member of the Jarvis household. Bryce assisted each of them up into the carriage. Her father—should she now think of him as her stepfather?—took his seat inside the landau carriage rather than in the front driver's seat. The roof was down. The Jarvises' carriage sat behind theirs, ready to return to their home.

Holly watched in silence as Bryce stepped up and sat in front. Calvin, her youngest brother, scrambled up and over the seat and snuggled next to Bryce. Bryce reached around and pulled Calvin closer. Holly's heart ached for her brothers and sister. Their lives would never be the same.

Tiffany snuggled into Holly. Holly embraced her and kissed the top of her head. "With God's grace we can do this, Tiff."

Tiffany nodded and cried. Her father reached into his inner coat pocket and pulled out a handkerchief. "We will all miss her, child. It is appropriate to shed tears."

"Oh, Papa." Tiffany leaped across the carriage floor to her father's arms.

"I miss her, too, darling." He cradled his fifteen-year-old daughter as if she were only five.

Holly found herself envious. If she weren't twenty she'd be in his lap, too, as she had been in his lap in the pri-

vacy of the den the day before. Her other brothers Daniel
and Riley snuggled in closer. Holly took a lace handkerchief from her purse and wiped her own eyes. At that
moment the band fell into place and marched behind the
carriages, playing some of mother's favorite hymns. Momma's words about God giving us strength through music
and joy floated back to Holly. A small, gentle smile lifted
her damp cheeks. Perhaps she could get through this horrible loss.

Emmett Landers' tombstone came back into view, her
real father's tombstone—a testimony to a man who wasn't
really dead. A man her mother loved.

Holly's heart ached for the loss her mother felt at the
death of her first husband. She couldn't imagine the shock
of discovering he was still alive after being told he was
dead. But why had Allison Graham left the tombstone in
the family plot, rather than have it removed once she'd
learned the truth?

Bryce reined in his emotions as he drove the carriage
back to the Graham estate. They went from one extreme
to another: fury at seeing Whit Butterfield at the graveside, protectiveness toward Holly and her family. Calvin
clutching at his side didn't help…and yet it did. He was
doing something. He could embrace the boy and share his
love and strength with him.

The grand two-story house came into view. Bryce led
the horses through the gate and pulled up to the front of
the house. He dismounted and helped Calvin climb down.
He assisted Holly who was dressed in black and white with
an Irish-laced shawl she more than likely had made. Then
he reached for Tiffany and each of her brothers. John Graham was the last to stand. "Thank you, Bryce."

"It is my honor, sir. I shall tend to the carriages and the horses."

"Again, I thank you, son."

Bryce nodded. He hopped back up on the carriage and pulled away from the walkway as his father's carriage pulled up and stopped. Most folks, he knew, wouldn't stay for long. They'd come in, nibble on some food, make their condolences and bid them goodbye. There would be a few who would linger until dark but, apart from his family and Allison Graham's parents, Bryce honestly didn't know who would stick around.

A few hours later Bryce had his answer. Widow Sullivan remained. He didn't know if she were shopping for a new husband or simply wanted to be there to encourage John Graham during his time of loss. If anyone understood the death of a spouse, it would be a widow or a widower.

As the guests departed, Holly's smile slipped. Bryce made his way over. "May I help you?"

"Yes, take me away from all of this."

"How about Venice?" he asked and winked. It was an old joke, a memory from their childhood. Venice was as far away from Savannah as they could imagine. Bryce hadn't let go of that treasured childhood dream—at least, not yet.

Holly giggled. "Venice sounds perfect."

He gave her his elbow. She hesitated for a moment then slipped her hand on top of his forearm. "Come away with me."

She stared into his eyes. For a brief moment he thought he saw desire in her incredible orbs. But they flickered back to the impenetrable emerald green he'd always known. "I am at your disposal."

He guided her out the back and onto the gazebo overlooking the river. "Tide is low."

"Apparently. Come sit with me for a moment."

Using all his skills as the gentleman host, he assisted her to the bench and stepped a pace away and sat. "How can I help, Holly?"

"I need a friend. No, I need more than that. I need a confidant. Someone I can share my deepest secrets with and who will not share them with another."

"I can do that. I may not have finished law school but I understand a commitment to confidence."

Holly smiled.

Bryce's heart beat wildly. Did this have to do with the trip she might need to take to Tennessee?

"I know you do. Forgive me but I…" She let her words drain off.

He closed the gap between them and placed his arm around her shoulders. "You can trust me, Holly."

Fresh tears welled in her eyes. "I am having a difficult time."

Naturally. He held back his meaningless quip.

"Momma, on the day she died, revealed something to me. I…"

Bryce waited and prayed for the Lord's direction and peace to cover Holly.

"Momma told me that John Graham is not my father."

Bryce stopped breathing.

"Good reserve, Bryce. I know you are stunned. So am I." She paused and held his gaze. Bryce kept his control and waited. "I thought she was delirious from the medicine and pain. But she wasn't. She left me three letters—I've only read one, her explanation to me." She quickly summarized what the letter had said.

Bryce's eyes widened. "Where is your father? Who is he?"

"His name is Emmett Landers and he lives in Tennessee. At least he did when he and my momma were married."

So, Father does know. He must be Emmett's attorney! "What do you want to do about all of this?"

"For one, I do not wish to tarnish my mother and father's reputation. I can see the gossipers humming with all of this."

Bryce released Holly. He stood and paced back and forth in the gazebo. Should he tell Holly his father is her real father's lawyer? No, that would be breaking Father's confidence. "Agreed. Does anyone else in your family know about this?"

"No. Just Father and I. Oh, and my grandparents. But they are not aware that I know, unless Father told them. I certainly didn't."

"How can I help?"

"Would you be with me when I read the letters from my father?"

"I would be honored. When would you like to read them?" Bryce had so many questions he wanted to ask his father, but that would be breaking Holly's confidence.

"Tomorrow. Will you still be assisting Father with the chores?"

"Yes but…" He paused. "Never mind. Tomorrow is perfect. What time?"

"Let's go for a carriage ride, pack a lunch, make a day out of it."

I'd love to. "What about your family? Will they be needing you close by?"

"Yes, I suppose so. Honestly, I am having a hard time focusing on anyone apart from myself. Your snuggling Calvin on the drive home caused me to reach over and embrace Tiffany. Normally I would have done that, but I am not myself."

"Holly, you have had quite a shock. It is normal. I am happy to read the letters with you, and I would love to simply spend a day with you. However, I would not be a good friend if I did not ask… Are you certain you want to confront these letters tomorrow? Would a day or two to relax and get back into the daily necessities be in order first?"

"That's just it, Bryce. I don't feel my life will ever be orderly again. I'm not who I thought I was. There's a stranger's blood running through my veins. I don't know what kind of character he has or what he looks like. Do I have any of his characteristics? Would my wanting to know my father hurt John? Do I even want to know a man who simply left me? I mean, couldn't he have found a way to be a part of my life? Did he even want me?"

Bryce closed the distance between them and clasped her hands, pulling her up. "We shall read his letters tomorrow. Those questions need to be answered for your peace of mind."

Holly enveloped Bryce into her embrace. "I've missed you, Bryce."

"I have missed you, too, Holly."

She lifted her head from his chest. "Why did you stay away?"

"I will tell you at another time. For now, let us deal with this incredible news."

Holly closed her eyes and rested in the strong arms of Bryce Jarvis. She found strength and a calmness there. They'd hugged many times over the years but tonight, and the day Mother died, were different. She eased out of his embrace. "I should be getting back to the house. There's so much to do."

He caught her arm. "My mother will take care of it, Holly. Stay for one more moment, please."

She paused. Had he felt the same emotions? Was their relationship about to change? Should it? He was her unofficial big brother. He'd given her advice about almost everything over the years—from how to ride a horse to how to know which boys to avoid. "What is it?"

"I just want you to know that I shall do whatever you need. Whatever, whenever."

She knitted her eyebrows then relaxed. "You are right, tonight is not the time to discuss anything further."

He flashed his incredible smile. She understood why his father had wanted him to be a lawyer. He could win over an entire jury box with that smile.

He escorted her back to the house. Inside she found the younger children were getting ready for bed. The older ones were cleaning up and finishing the dishes.

A gentle rap on the door caught everyone's attention. Who could be arriving at such a late hour?

Bryce stepped forward and greeted the man. "Good evening, may I help you?"

"I came to pay my respects. Forgive me for the late hour. My train was delayed in Augusta. Is John Graham here?"

"Yes, sir. May I ask who's calling?" Bryce asked.

"Emmett Landers."

Holly's face flushed hot, then cold. The room swirled.

Chapter 3

Bryce caught Holly before her head hit the floor. He gathered her in his arms and carried her to the sofa.

"Chad, take your brothers home. Your mother and I will join you shortly," his father ordered. He extended his hand to Emmett Landers. "It's good to see you, old friend."

John cleared his throat. "Old friend?"

"Yes, John. Emmett and I attended college together."

Bryce watched John Graham control his emotions, then turn to his daughter. "Tiffany, would you make certain your brothers are down for the evening?"

"Yes, sir." Tiffany gathered her soft blue dress and walked up the stairs. The room was empty of all the younger children.

"I didn't mean to intrude, John. I tried to get here in time for the funeral."

"I'm not angry with you, Emmett. At this point I would not know my best friend."

Bryce stood. "Gentlemen, Mother, let's sit down. Holly spoke with me earlier this evening, so I am aware of whom you are, Mr. Landers."

Emmett Landers' shoulders relaxed. He had strong shoulders and a body that said he did a lot of physical labor.

"Lloyd, why did you keep this from me?" John asked. "I mean, you knew about Emmett from Allison and me. Why keep your knowledge of Emmett a secret?"

"Attorney-client confidentiality, John."

Holly moaned. Bryce knelt beside her. His mother handed him a glass of water. "Thank you."

"Holly learned yesterday who you are, Emmett," John offered.

Emmett Landers sat in the rocker. "Ah. Has she read my letter?"

"No, sir," Bryce answered. "Not yet."

Holly's eyelids blinked open. "Can we go to Venice now?"

"Absolutely." Bryce smiled.

"Venice?" The older adults echoed one another.

Holly sat up.

"Sip this." Bryce handed her the tall glass of cool water.

"Thank you." She sipped and scanned the others staring at her… Her father, Bryce's parents and her other father. Her gaze lingered. "You are Emmett Landers?"

"Yes, and everyone in this room knows who I am."

"Let's tell the whole world! Shout it from the mountaintops. I have lived all my life believing a lie. Venice is sounding better by the moment."

"Holly, I came to pay my respects. I did not intend to play havoc with your life. Is this young man your fiancé? Lloyd, is this your oldest son?"

"No, Emmett, we are good friends of the Graham family. Holly, your father is my client," Lloyd clarified.

"You mean, both of my fathers are your clients?"

"Yes, I suppose that is true. Emmett had me draw up the annulment for his and Allison's marriage."

John looked over at Lloyd and raised his eyebrow, then relaxed his shoulders. "Forgive me for getting angry, Lloyd. It was not the best day to hear such news."

Holly jumped up at that. "I cannot believe all of you. Does anyone have any idea how much this is hurting me? I lost my mother, and all I can think about is that I really didn't know her. I have a father I never knew, who happens to have an empty grave in the cemetery where we buried my mother today."

Holly shook her head, trying to clear the fog in her mind. "And then Momma was stuck between two men she loved and my first father decided to walk away from us, from me—only to return now. And I ought to believe that he cares for me? No word, not one single word!" Holly paced back and forth. "Take me to Venice, Bryce, please."

Bryce came up beside her and wrapped her in his arms. "Excuse us." Bryce led Holly out of the room, through the great hall and out the front door. They were in the carriage house in no time at all. "Holly, I shall take you wherever you want to go. However, I think now is not that time to run away from your past."

"I know you are right. I don't want to run away. I just need some time to absorb all this. So, your father has known this secret."

"Apparently. Before the funeral today he asked me to clear my schedule and be ready to escort you on a possible trip to Tennessee. I need a few days to put my business affairs in order but after that I will be free to do whatever you need me to do."

"Just be here for me, Bryce. I need a friend."

"You know you can count on me." He led her to a stack

of hay bales and encouraged her to sit. "Would you like me to ready a carriage for a moonlight ride?" He bowed at the waist and pretended to remove an invisible cap. "My lady."

Holly giggled despite herself. "No, thank you. I will face them in a few minutes. I want to figure out what I am going to do."

"Nothing." Bryce sat beside her. "Please understand… I am in the dark as much as you. But here is what I see went on. I am going to call everyone by their first names because 'my father,' 'your father' and 'fathers' is confusing."

Holly agreed with a nod of the head.

"Emmett must have gone to his college friend, Lloyd, for legal advice about his marriage to Allison. Lloyd obviously drew up the annulment, and over the years he has been in touch with Emmett. How and why is a mystery at this point. My father…excuse me…Lloyd, being a man who will not break a confidence even for his good friends, never would have told John that Emmett was his client, even though at some point in time they must have changed your legal name to Graham."

"You mean, my name might not be Graham? I suppose that is possible. Holly Landers. It doesn't roll off the tongue quite as easily as Graham. Who am I?"

"You are who you have always been."

"I do not feel that way."

"Holly, give yourself some time to adjust to all this news. I myself am stunned, and it is not happening to me. And your beloved mother has just passed. I cannot imagine what you have been going through. I also believe that all four parents in there do care about you and are concerned for you."

Holly sighed. "I know. And Momma said she loved Emmett and could not choose between him and John. I cannot imagine being forced to make that kind of a decision."

"Nor I. On the other hand, Emmett seems to be a man of honor to sacrifice his wife and daughter for their best interest. From what I know of law, your mother and John's marriage would not have been legal. The first marriage would be in effect. Emmett could have forced his wife to leave her second husband and return to Tennessee with him."

"Poor Momma."

"Your poor father. Can you imagine such a sacrifice?"

"No. My heart would be breaking."

"As would mine. He must be quite a man."

"And all I did was yell at him."

Bryce chuckled. "I imagine your father Emmett would have seen that temper a time or two from your mom."

Despite her grief and confusion, Holly laughed and swatted him on the shoulder.

Bryce rubbed it out. "You are the spitting image of your mother. Emmett must be experiencing déjà vu seeing you."

"They must have been married at my age now," Holly added. She leaned back against the bales of hay. The fresh-cut scent reminded her of the harvest. "Even if I somehow muster the courage to survive the next days, I think we might want to consider planning a trip to Venice. The idea of floating down the canals with a gondolier guiding us through the water streets sounds heavenly."

Bryce leaned back on the hay. "Yes, it does. I would be happy to take you to Venice, under one condition."

"What's that?"

"You go as my wife."

Holly's eyes widened. Bryce couldn't believe he'd said the words out loud. He wouldn't take them back. "Holly, I asked your father to court you a couple years ago after I returned from college. He asked me to wait until you were twenty-one. This is why I haven't been around much the past couple of years. I knew that if I spent any amount of time speaking with you, I would blurt out my desires."

Holly smiled. Her eyes lit with excitement. "I am honored, and I would court you, even possibly marry you if my mother hadn't just passed away. I need time, Bryce."

"I know, and I won't ask again until you tell me you are ready to answer the question, or you tell me to find another wife."

Holly's eyes widened. He pressed his finger to her lips. "Relax, Holly. I am not proposing marriage just yet." He winked.

"You understand me well."

"Shall we return and put those poor folks out of their misery?"

"Yes. But truthfully, I'd rather have them squirm for a bit longer."

"They all know you. Emmett will, in time. You are quick to anger, yet let it go as easily as it flares up."

"True."

Bryce stood and offered his assistance.

"Shall we tell them we are engaged?" Holly teased.

"Not until I have had a chance to kiss you. Seems we have never gotten around to trying that."

Holly turned and faced him. She closed her eyes and leaned into him.

He placed his hands firmly on her shoulders and eased her away from him. "No, Holly, I will not kiss you tonight. When I kiss you it will be when there is no question in either of our minds. Tonight you are reacting from the loss of your mother, the confusion of meeting a father you never knew existed...not a love or desire for me."

She opened her eyes and focused. "Thank you. I will need your strength. Forgive me. I am questioning God and His decisions."

He led her back to the house. "Understandable. However, I shall pray for you."

"Thank you, Bryce. I don't believe I could make it through all of this without you."

"I am honored. Shall we?" He held the door open for them to enter the great hall. Inside the sitting room they found their parents mourning the loss of Allison and worried about the turn of events that had impacted Holly. He pulled a straw of hay from Holly's hair.

John Graham narrowed his gaze on Bryce. Bryce wanted to pull at the collar of his shirt and give his neck more breathable space.

"Forgive my outburst," Holly offered. She turned to Emmett Landers. "And forgive me. I have not read your letter yet."

"I understand. It has not been easy for me, either, but I have made a life for myself, and have a wife, and you have some additional brothers and sisters, as well. Mr. Jarvis has a packet of letters that were to be given to you on your twenty-first birthday but, given the circumstances, you may have them as soon as you are up to reading them." Emmett Landers stood. "I shall depart for the evening. I will find a room in one of the hotels and send word as to where you can find me. I would enjoy a visit with you at some point, but only when you are ready. But know that I cannot stay long. I shall be in Savannah for two days. Lloyd and I have some business to attend to, as well."

"You are welcome to stay here, Emmett," John offered. Holly knew the gesture had to be difficult, but he was a good man. "There is plenty of room."

"Holly?" Emmett asked.

"That would be fine."

"Then I accept. Thank you, John."

"Bryce, your mother and I are going to return home.

Holly, Mrs. Jarvis will return in the morning and help with whatever is needed. Give yourself a couple of days to recover from your loss and this sudden knowledge."

"Thank you. Thank you both. You have been so kind to us."

"Our pleasure." Cynthia Jarvis smiled and gave Holly a very motherly embrace. "I will be here first light. Do not fret about a thing."

Holly sat on the chair next to her bed with Momma's Bible on her lap. Inside were the two letters she still had to read. A part of her wanted to read them now, while another wanted to wait for Bryce. She traced the spine of the Bible with her finger then set it on the nightstand.

Instead, she reached for the book *Italy, Florence and Venice* by the French writer Hippolyte Taine and translated by John Durand. She opened to the worn bookmark, a token Bryce had made for her many years ago when she'd turned thirteen. She fingered the thin strip of leather, where Bryce had carefully hand-tooled holly leaves and berries on the front. She scanned down to the familiar passage.

April 21—A day in a gondola. It is necessary to wander about and see the whole.

Venice is the pearl of Italy. I have seen nothing equal to it. I know of but one city that approaches it—very remotely, and only on account of its architecture—and that is, Oxford…

Her eyes drifted down to the familiar words and settled on…

For the first time one admires not only with the brain, but also with the heart, the senses and the entire being. One feels fully disposed to be happy; one confesses that life is beautiful and good. All that is essential is to open the eyes, there being no need of effort; the gondola glides along insensibly, and, reclining in it, one wholly abandons himself physically and mentally. A bland and gentle breeze caresses the cheeks. The broad surface of the canal undulates with the rosy and white forms of the palaces asleep in the freshness and silence of dawn; everything is forgotten, profession, projects, self; one gazes, becomes absorbed, and revels as if suddenly released from life and soaring aerially above all things in light and in azure.

Holly closed her eyes and imagined the rest as the writer took the reader down the Grand Canal and through the various sights and sounds that made up this truly unique city of islands, marble and waterways. To be on a gondola and let life's problems float away… How much would she give to have that peace in her life right now? To forget the past, the present and not even entertain a thought for her future. Was it normal to feel this way? Did the death of a parent cause one to want to flee? Or was it the disorienting deathbed confession of her mother?

A knot the size of a pecan hardened in the pit of her stomach. She replaced the leather bookmark, stood and returned the book to the shelf and shuffled numbly to her bedroom window. She stood there, paralyzed for a moment, uncertain as to whether or not to give in to her physical body and sleep, or to push away the haziness and grasp the reality of her life.

Dawn's first light peaked a golden glow over the horizon. A foggy mist blanketed the calm water of the river. A new day was beginning. "Momma, I miss you. I wish you had told me years ago. Then perhaps you could have helped me through this. I know you said in your letter you hoped I would understand. But I don't. I wish I did but…" She paused, not wanting to speak out loud words she would regret, even if they were spoken in the silence of her room.

A distant memory of being alone at the water's edge and watching an alligator swim past came into focus. She'd been told they were dangerous and to stay away from the water's edge. But at four, and feeling very much assured in her own abilities, she'd faced the creature. She'd known even at that early age that their skin was like soft leather, and she loved the feel of it. What would be so wrong in petting an alligator? she'd reasoned. She'd looked over her shoulders and put on her rubber boots, then taken a single step into the marsh.

"Holly Elizabeth Landers, you come back right this very moment!" Momma's voice had reprimanded.

She *was* a Landers! When did she become a Graham? Had she, legally? Holly closed her eyes and collapsed on her bed. "This is too much, God. Why?"

Chapter 4

Bryce finished the notes for his brothers regarding the oversight of operations for the plantation. He'd worked late into the night to be available for Holly. He closed the lid of the drop-front mahogany secretary. He'd had the desk designed with the same wood and hand-carved moldings as his father's desk. Bryce's desk gave him a small area to keep the papers pertaining to the operation of the plantation separate from his father's legal and family papers. He slipped the key into his pocket and turned at the voice of his mother. "You're up bright and early this morning, son. How are you?" His mother leaned against the doorway with a mug of coffee in her hand.

"Fine. That smells good."

"I made a full pot. Did you sleep?"

"I managed a few hours. I take it you knew all about Holly and her family?"

She stepped farther into the room. "I knew John wasn't

her biological father, yes. And I knew Emmett Landers was her real father. I didn't know about the letters or the reasons for keeping Holly in the dark."

Bryce stood, walked around to the front of his father's desk and leaned against it.

"How is she doing?" She took another step into the home office and sipped her coffee.

"This information didn't surface at a good time. I cannot imagine dealing with the loss of a parent and discovering that kind of news. I am your son, right?"

His mother smiled as she sat in the soft-cushioned sofa and arranged her nightgown and robe. "Yes, you are my son and your father's."

"Well, I knew I was his, we have too many similar features."

"That you do." She winked and took another sip.

"Do you have any idea why Allison Graham would have chosen to keep this information a secret from Holly?"

"I'm afraid not. It was a subject Allison never wanted to talk about. I do know from your father that John was quite concerned he'd lose Allison to Emmett when he returned from the war. She truly loved Emmett. But she loved John, too, for that matter. I cannot imagine being forced to choose."

"Nor I." Bryce raked his hair back from his face. "Mother, I want to do right by Holly but she is so vulnerable right now. It is going to take all of my strength and willpower not to succumb to my own desires. I almost asked her to marry me last night. It is a blur. I do remember promising that I would take her to Venice under one condition, that she'd come as my wife."

He heard a sharp intake of breath from his mother and caught her gaze.

"It was more of a tease, but truth is truth. I do love her

and I do want her to be my bride, but this is not the time to ask, or act."

"Be patient, son. There will be a time and a place. You know the passage in Ecclesiastes 3:1. 'To every thing there is a season, and a time to every purpose under the heaven.' I cannot speak to God's timing but I do know from the few short years I have lived, that ultimately God's timing and purpose is best."

"Yes, but is this God's timing or man's? Do the careless actions of Whit Butterfield equal God's plans or did man interrupt God's perfect plan?"

She placed her coffee mug down and motioned for him to take a seat beside her. "I cannot say what happened the other day with Mr. Butterfield was God's perfect plan for Allison, but I do know that God was very aware of what would happen. Why He allows people to make mistakes that harm themselves or others, I do not know or understand. But I do know that He is a God of comfort and compassion and He will give Holly and us the peace we are looking for during this tragedy."

Bryce clasped his hands together and bent his head. "I know, but I am still dealing with my anger toward Whit, even though it wasn't all his fault."

"I understand. But remember, my son, Whit is suffering, as well. I cannot imagine being responsible for someone's death and having to live with that kind of knowledge."

Bryce pulled his gaze from his hands to his mother's face. He knew how she mourned Allison Graham, her closest friend and confidante. And yet in her eyes he saw compassion for Whit. Somehow, she could forgive him.

How? *God's grace.* The answer flew into his mind the moment he thought the question. Followed by the image of him extending his hand to Whit Butterfield in kindness and compassion.

"What's the matter, dear?"

"Nothing. Just something I remembered I should do."

"Oh, all right then. I am going to get dressed for the day. I will ride with you to the Grahams."

"I shall have the carriage ready." Bryce stood and followed his mother out of the room, watching as she ascended the stairs.

A knock at the front door pushed him back into a man of action. Opening the door, his hand tightened on the knob. Not in a million years would he expect to see this person standing at his door.

"Hello, Bryce."

Holly woke to the gentle knocking on her door. "Holly?"

"Tiff, what time is it?"

"Ten. Papa thought I should check on you."

Holly bolted up from the bed and straightened her nightclothes. "Tell Father I'll be down in a moment."

"All right." Tiffany turned and paused. "Holly, who is Emmett Landers?"

She debated whether to confide in Tiffany. The truth would need to come out sometime. Should she be the one to tell? Yes, yes, she should. It was her life, her parentage, and too many secrets had been kept. "My father."

"Pardon?"

Tiffany listened with despair as Holly recited what she understood so far. "What are you going to do? Are you going to move away and live with your father?"

"I don't know. I have many questions and both our fathers are the only ones who can give me the answers. Please don't tell the boys yet. They may not understand all of this."

Tiffany came and sat on Holly's bed. "I don't know what to think. You never knew?"

"I recalled a childhood memory late last night, or rather, early this morning. I remember being four years old and at the water's edge and Momma calling me back to the house using all three of my names. Holly Elizabeth Landers."

"If we were in trouble Momma always did that." Tiffany smiled. "So she called you Landers, not Graham, in this memory?"

"Yes, so I guess way down deep I knew the truth. Most of my memories start from about five years old."

"So do mine. You've always been my big sister."

"And I will always be your big sister, there is no changing that. We might have different fathers, but we have the same mother."

"Yes, but you got Momma's looks and I got Father's complexion."

"Be glad for that, you don't burn like I do in the Savannah sun."

"True, but I always loved your and Momma's green eyes. Mine are just brown, plain old brown."

Holly sat on the bed next to her sister. "You are a beautiful young woman, Tiff, remember that."

"Oh, I know I'm pretty. The boys at school tell me all the time." Tiffany grinned, half joking.

"And do I need to report this to Father?"

"Don't you dare. I like the attention. Momma told me to be careful."

"And I'll second that. Wait until you are older before you consider courting."

"Well, I'm not going to wait until I'm twenty-one, that's just too old. I guess I see now why Momma and Papa didn't want you to get involved with anyone before you were twenty-one, but why did they decide to wait so long to tell you? Wouldn't it have been wiser to tell you when, perhaps, you were sixteen or eighteen even?"

"That's another question I don't have the answer to, but I aim to find out." Holly got up and decided to dress while chatting with her sister. She walked behind the dressing wall and removed her nightgown.

"I cannot imagine what it would be like to learn this. What are you going to do? Marry Bryce and run away to Venice?"

Holly popped her head around the partition. "Were you listening last night?"

Tiffany blushed. "A little. So, are you and Bryce going to Venice?"

"No."

"Are you going to marry him?"

"Did you go to the barn last night, too?"

Tiffany giggled. "No. What happened in the barn?"

"Nothing." Holly felt the heat of her own blush. Not looking into the mirror, she suspected her blush to be about three times darker than Tiffany's.

"Did you kiss him? He likes you, you know. When you're not looking he's always staring at you."

"He is?" Holly paused buttoning her blue blouse.

"Uh-huh. I heard him ask Papa to court you a couple of years ago."

"You are a little eavesdropper, aren't you?" Her hands shook as she buttoned the next button.

"Maybe. I just hear things. People don't always look when they are speaking. Last night I was listening, though."

Holly decided not to ask any further questions regarding Bryce. "How are Father and the boys today?"

"I think we are all still overwhelmed by Momma being gone. Mrs. Jarvis has been cooking and cleaning all morning. But I saw her wiping away tears, too. She and Momma were good friends."

"Yes, they were." Holly finished dressing then stood in front of her mirror and brushed out her hair.

Tiffany came up behind her. "Sit and allow me."

Holly handed the hairbrush to her sister and sat. "Thank you."

"You're welcome. So, you didn't sleep well?"

"No, too much on my mind."

"Me, neither. I kept crying and thinking about Momma and how much I was going to miss her."

"Me, too." Holly closed her eyes and remembered her mother's hands going through her hair. She smiled and opened her eyes, looking into the mirror and into her sister's deep brown eyes. "You have Momma's touch. You brush my hair the same way Momma did."

Tiffany smiled. "I loved the way she brushed my hair."

"Me, too."

The sisters continued brushing and losing themselves to the memories of their mother. Holly felt closer to Mother having Tiffany's fingers combing through her hair. "Marvelous job, Tiff."

"Thank you. It's all in the wrists." They giggled together. Holly rose and wrapped her arm around her sister's shoulders. "It's time for us both to go and meet my father."

"How strange is that?" Tiffany said and followed in step with her sister. "Even though you've told me, I still cannot believe you aren't Papa's daughter."

"Oh, I am his daughter. He raised me. He'll always be my father. I just have two now."

Tiffany laughed. "Some people have all the luck."

Unable to stop herself, Holly laughed all the way down the stairs. Seeing her two fathers standing at the front door smothered the gaiety.

"Good morning, Fathers. I apologize for sleeping late."

John Graham's mouth gaped open.

Holly held down a dangerous smile. "I told Tiffany this morning." Her stepfather nodded. Emmett Landers nodded with a slight turn of the head. *Does my father have the same willful spirit?* "Is there any breakfast left?"

"Mrs. Jarvis saved a plate for you in the kitchen. We were about to take a walk around the property. Would you like to join us?" John offered.

"No, thank you. I will visit with Father Landers... With...Mr. Landers later. It will give Bryce and me a chance to go over the other letters."

"Letters?" Tiffany inquired.

"We will talk later, Tiffany. Right now I need to eat."

Tiffany smiled. "I look forward to it. I don't have to go to school today, but I must write my book report."

The men retreated out the door. Holly could tell they were as nervous as she. Tiffany ran back up the stairs and Holly headed into the kitchen. The fresh smell of baking bread filled the room.

"Good morning, Mrs. Jarvis."

"Good morning to you, child. How did you sleep?"

"Not very well. The sun was coming up over the horizon by the time I started to slumber."

"You set yourself right down and I will serve you. I made some fresh berry juice. Would you like some?"

"Yes, thank you." Holly sat at the small maple table in the kitchen. "Is Bryce here?"

"Out in the barn. He said to let him know when you woke."

Mrs. Jarvis placed the warm plate in front of her. A couple slices of French toast with a pool of butter on top stood proudly in the center. Next to that were three slices of bacon. She also placed a gravy boat with hot cane syrup beside her plate. "Coffee, tea?"

"Tea, thank you."

"I will have the juice in a moment."

Holly lowered her head and silently offered a brief prayer of thanks for the food. She paused then poured the hot syrup.

The back door squeaked open. Bryce stood in the doorway. "I will fix that squeak later. How are you?" He smiled. He looked as tired as she felt. But he was still…handsome. Six feet tall, with broad shoulders and the most comfortable chest to snuggle into…

Holly quelled her impure thoughts and went back to her breakfast.

"Awake," she answered. "You look like you didn't get much sleep, either."

"I had some work to do." He stepped up to the sink and washed his hands.

Mrs. Jarvis placed the juice in front of Holly. "Can I get you something, son?"

"Coffee, thanks." She nodded and he sat beside Holly. "How did you sleep?"

"Not well, I fell asleep around dawn."

"I was up before. I had an interesting visitor this morning."

"Oh?" Holly continued to eat her breakfast. It looked and smelled great but she noticed it had little taste. Food and health were important so she would continue to eat even though food had lost its flavor.

"An old schoolmate of mine. His name is Henry Rushton. He hails from Augusta, sailed down the river on his father's old plantation pole boat. He said he was on vacation, resting and relaxing after a hard summer and taking some time off before the harvest. He converted the boat so it has a long narrow room with a bed and a small kitchen."

"How's he going to move it upstream?"

"Apparently he put a small steam engine on it. It won't go too fast, but enough to go up the Savannah River."

Mrs. Jarvis handed her son his coffee.

"Are you up for reading the letters with me this morning?" she asked, hoping he still wanted to.

"If that is your wish."

"I have no choice. My father is here and I need to know what is in those two letters before I can even consider speaking with him."

Bryce nodded and sipped his coffee.

"I told Tiffany this morning. I realize my parents had a reason for keeping this a secret, and I am not inclined to telling the entire city, but I don't feel it is right to keep the family in the dark."

Bryce placed his mug on the table and cupped it with both hands. He blinked with tired eyes. His honey-brown eyes penetrated her foggy mind. Confidence and trust shone deeply into his soul. Yes, she'd picked the right person to help her wade through the confusion that overshadowed her life.

Only her mother would have been better. If only they'd been blessed with more time together....

Holly pushed the plate away. She couldn't continue to eat. She stood and grabbed Bryce's hand. "Come on, let's get this over with."

Chapter 5

Bryce held Holly's hand and followed her up the stairs to her room. A room he'd been in many times before. He stopped at her doorway. "I'll wait here. You fetch the letters and we'll read them in your father's den."

"I'm not concerned about my honor. You're like my big brother."

He wondered if she would ever see him as a possible suitor. "But I am not. Holly, let's do this right. There is no sense in giving tongues a chance to wag for no reason or purpose. Your father's den is appropriate and private."

She blushed. "You are right, thank you. I shall be just a moment." She slipped behind her bedroom door and Bryce turned to face the hallway. How many times had he run up and down these halls in the past? The second floor wrapped around the grand room with a walkway that encircled it. Each walkway had a hallway to the back of the building, where Holly's room sat, facing east and overlooking the river below.

The door clicked open. "Here, you hold them." She passed the two letters into his hand. He placed the yellowed envelopes in his breast pocket and without a word followed her down the hall and stairs.

He led her to the den and left the door ajar. Holly sat in the high-backed chair. He sat in the chair to her left. The room nearly mirrored that of his father's den, with slightly different furnishing but the same layout. "Would you like me to read them out loud or do you wish to read them silently to yourself?"

"Please give me Mother's letter first. I'll read it out loud."

He handed the open envelope that had Allison's name on it and placed the other back in his pocket.

"'Dear Allie,'" she began, her voice cracking.

"I am writing for you to understand my heart. I have decided to annul our marriage so that you can stay married to John Graham. My heart aches knowing that you believed I had died in the war. I was thoughtless in not sending you missives over the years. Perhaps one or two would have gotten through and let you know that I was still alive. I apologize. I love you with all my heart and soul."

Holly gasped. Her hands started to shake. Bryce wanted to cuddle her in his embrace but held back.

Holly continued.

"It is because of my love for you and Holly that I am doing this. I see your love for John Graham, and I see his love for you and Holly. I will miss you not being a part of my life, but I will miss not having the opportunity to be a part of our daughter's life most of all."

Holly wiped a tear from her eye then took in a deep pull of air.

"As you are well aware, I live in Tennessee. That is where our home is. I cannot take a child away from her mother so I will relinquish my rights for her sake. She calls John 'Daddy.' Oh how my heart ached when I heard that. I would not want to confuse her. I trust you will tell her when the time is right. She is the spitting image of you and oh so beautiful. My heart leaped in my chest just being able to embrace her for a moment."

Holly's voice wavered.

"I am giving you a letter to give to Holly. I may never see my daughter again in this life but I do want her to know that I love her."

Holly's hands were shaking so much the letter seemed to blow in the wind, but she continued.

"Please understand that if ever you need me, I will come. I will go on with my life and, if the good Lord allows, perhaps I shall find another wife. I am sorry I did not put you first. And I apologize for the pain you went through thinking I had been lost in the war. My heart aches for you, Allie. I love you and will love you forever. John is a good man, from what I've seen. God Bless you both.
All my love,
Emmett."

Bryce held his breath waiting for a response from Holly. She appeared to read the letter again. He could see himself in Emmett's shoes. He gave the impression of an honorable man, admitting failure and giving up his wife and child. But why would he move back to Tennessee? What would keep him so far away from his daughter?

Tears rolled down Holly's cheeks. Bryce reached into his pocket and pulled out a clean handkerchief. He had come prepared with three. "Here."

Holly turned and gazed into his eyes. "I cannot imagine giving up my family. I think I understand why but…"

Bryce reached out and held her hand. A few red strands of hair fell forward into her face. He wanted to brush them behind her ear but resisted the urge.

"I don't understand why he would give me up. I mean, I understand not taking a child from her mother, but why didn't he find work in Savannah, make a life here? At least be a part of my life."

"Perhaps his letter to you explains in more detail."

"Perhaps, but he wrote this letter to a five-year-old. I doubt he put much thought into the reasons for not staying in a letter he didn't know when I would read."

"True, but he did know it would be when you were older."

"Are you certain you aren't on his side?"

"I am not taking sides, Holly. I am thinking he had his reasons for backing away. He gave a couple of those reasons in the letter to your mother. Or perhaps those were the entirety of his reasons. We do not know. But you do have the advantage of asking him while he is here."

Holly leaned back in the chair and closed her eyes. "A part of me would like to ask him all the questions popping up in my head. Another part of me is afraid."

"Afraid? How so?"

"I don't know if I can explain it, really. It is a fear, I suppose, but one that comes from this feeling of rejection I've been dealing with since I first learned the news. I can see from his letter his leaving us was a noble gesture, but I still feel slighted. I feel he didn't really care about me, that if he really cared he would have stayed in Savannah."

"That wasn't an option," John Graham interrupted from the doorway.

Startled, Holly turned toward the unexpected voice. "Why not?" she inquired.

John walked into the den. Behind him stood Emmett Landers. "I suppose I should answer that question." Emmett spoke just above a whisper.

Holly simply nodded. Emmett's large, taut frame consumed a surprising portion of the doorway, his head nearly touching the lintel. He held the wide brim of a rancher's hat in a gentle grip between strong, heavily veined hands. Kind eyes set within a tanned face accustomed to long hours in the open air stared back at her, unflinching, beckoning....

"Allie's biggest concern was for you, Holly." The warmth of his voice reached a deep place within her. "You had been told your daddy died in the war. She was concerned about how you would react. Your mother had recently married, and apparently it took you six months before you called John 'Daddy.' She didn't want to confuse you. If I lived here, you would be quite confused for a while about who was your father. Granted, as you got older you would have managed but..." Emmett let his words trail off. "Suffice it to say, we felt it best at the time."

She looked to her stepfather to confirm her father's words. John nodded.

"I never wanted to leave you, Holly, but I made my peace with this decision fifteen years ago. I understand your confusion and your feelings of rejection. I am here now and will answer any question you have, no matter how difficult. I believe it is best for us not to keep any secrets and to be open and honest about the good and the bad regarding this decision. John and I have discussed it, as well. He is in agreement."

Holly turned to John Graham. "Are you, Father?"

"Yes, but with hesitation. Bryce, would you please leave us?"

Bryce stood. Holly grabbed hold of his wrist. "Wait. Father, I know you are a private man but Bryce is…"

"Holly, I shall stay if you wish, but you are safe with your fathers."

"I know I am safe. I'm uncertain as to whether or not I can control my temper."

"Holly Elizabeth! For what purpose would your temper serve at this moment?" John chastised.

Holly glared at him. Bryce wrapped her in his arms. He felt her relax. "Mr. Graham, I will not speak of anything that is said to anyone outside of this room. But I believe Holly requires some support, and for reasons I do not understand but am grateful for, she has chosen me."

John Graham collapsed in the chair behind his desk. "Very well. I don't cotton to having other people know our business."

Emmett sat in the chair Bryce had been sitting in earlier. He wrung his hat in his hands. "Holly, I will answer all your questions." His words were softly spoken and Bryce again felt her body relax even more.

"Forgive me…Fathers, but you must understand one thing about all of this. I do not know who I am. My world is in total chaos. Not only have I lost my mother but I am not who I've thought myself to be. I am curious how a man could leave his child." She turned to Emmett Landers. "I know by your letter to Mother that you didn't abandon us, but I still feel that you did."

Emmett wrung his hat tighter. "I understand, and I cannot change the past. Your mother and I did what we thought was best at the time. Only you can accept our choices or not. Please understand I do love you. You've been a constant part of my daily thoughts. Which is why Lloyd Jarvis has a bundle of letters from me to you."

"But why Tennessee?"

"It was family land and something your mother and I worked hard to acquire, and I've worked many long hours to bring life from it. It's a horse and cattle ranch and has tripled in size since you and your mother left. My roots were there, not here in Savannah."

Bryce massaged her shoulders. "I would like to say I understand but…" She paused.

"It's too soon," Emmett proposed. "Like I said, I've had this knowledge and have lived with my decision for fifteen years. I'd love to say there hasn't been a day when I didn't regret my decision, but that wouldn't be the truth. There were a few days here and there, but overall I was at peace with it. Seeing the hurt in your eyes, I do have my doubts. I am sorry for the pain, daughter. It was not our intent."

"Thank you."

Bryce observed John Graham and how he watched Emmett and Holly. Did fear of losing Holly worry Mr. Graham?

She turned in Bryce's arms and faced him. "Will you make a carriage ready for us?"

"At your service, my lady." Bryce winked and left her there with her fathers.

Holly turned to the two men representing all the confusion that now defined her life. "I don't mean to be disrespectful to either of you, but I am having a hard time with all of this." She turned toward Emmett Landers. "I cannot say that I fully understand why you chose to do what you did. I do understand that at the moment you thought you were doing what was in my best interest."

She turned to her stepfather. "And I understand that you and Mother wanted to wait until I was older. But I am sorry, twenty-one seems a bit old to me. I could understand sixteen, possibly as late as seventeen, after I graduated from school. But why wait until I was twenty-one?"

"It was the age when your mother and I started courting," John whispered.

She turned back to Emmett. "How old was my mother when you and she married?"

"Seventeen. Right after she finished her schooling."

She turned back to John. "Why would you feel I had to wait until twenty-one when my mother married Emmett at seventeen?"

"She and I both felt she was impulsive at that time. That perhaps, if she had waited a bit longer, she wouldn't have..." His words trailed off.

"That she wouldn't have married me?" Emmett stood. "Did you try to convince Allison that our relationship wasn't genuine because we were young?"

"Not exactly. It doesn't matter what Allison and I discussed."

Holly stood. "Yes, it does, Father. However, I am not going to be a part of the two of you fighting about the past. Father Emmett..." She turned to him. "I'll want to visit with you again after I return from my outing with Bryce." She turned to John. "And I'll be home when I've had enough time to digest everything I've heard and read this morning. Father, I love you but I sense there was..." Holly didn't want to say it out loud, let alone believe, that her stepfather had had a hand in her not knowing her real father all these years.

"We did what we thought best, Holly," John mumbled.

"So you keep saying. For what it is worth, Father Emmett, early this morning I recalled my mother calling me Holly Elizabeth Landers. I was only four at the time." She turned back to John. "Am I a Landers or legally a Graham?"

"Legally, a Landers. Emmett wouldn't sign the papers for me to adopt you."

She turned to Emmett, the unspoken question hanging in the tense air.

"You are my daughter. If you could only have a small part of me, I wanted it to be my name."

She faced John again. "And you have led me to believe I was a Graham all this time, knowing my name was Landers?"

John looked down at his lap. "Yes. Perhaps that was wrong of me but…"

Holly held up her hand. "You say you were doing what you thought was best for me. Did it not even occur to you that everyone who attended your wedding knew Mother had been married once before, and that I was there as living proof?"

He gave no reaction.

"I don't understand the secrecy. Why? The entire city knows. Everyone knew except the one person it actually mattered to—me. I did not know. Does that not seem even vaguely unfair to you?"

"I'm sorry, Holly. We…" This time he held back from saying the line that blazed in her memory.

We did what we thought best.

She let out a deep sigh. "Bryce and I will be home around dinnertime. Don't wait on us. Bryce said an old college friend was in the area. Perhaps we'll go out to dinner with him. It is certainly time for some distraction of a sort. My head is spinning."

Emmett extended his hand, palm up. Holly placed hers inside his. "All of us wanted what was best. I understand your confusion, Holly. Please know that everyone involved thought of you first. Perhaps we made some mistakes, but our intentions were in the right place." He gave her hand a gentle squeeze.

"I know. If you do not mind, we will stop by Mr. Jarvis's office and pick up the other letters."

A smile raised on Emmett's face that brought a sparkle to his blue eyes. "I'd like that."

And for the first time that she could remember, she leaned into the man who was her flesh and blood and gave him a hug. Being in his arms, accepting his love, felt familiar and yet, somehow, entirely new. He held her tighter and kissed her cheek. "I love you, pumpkin. I always have and I always will," he whispered.

She pulled away, seeing the pain in John Graham's eyes. She was still unsure of her true identity, but knew one thing: both men in this room did love her in their own unique way.

Outside she found Bryce ready with the hooded buggy. "Where are we headed, my lady?" he asked with a bow.

"To your father's office, if that is where my letters are."

He assisted her up to the only seat. "I think John Graham was behind my not knowing about all of this until I was twenty-one. He said they'd decided on that age because that was the age when he and my mother started courting."

Bryce gathered the reins and motioned for the horse to go forward. "I agree, John is holding something back. Of course, your father has always been reserved, so I do not want to overspeculate as to his reasons."

"Yes, he is a private man. Still, can't he see that the only person they had been deceiving was me? Everyone had to have known Mother was a widow and that I was the child from that marriage. Oh, and by the way, I am a Landers, even if my graduation certificate from school says Graham on it." She related what had transpired after Bryce had left the room.

"Again, the deception. I reckon since they decided not to tell you that you had a different father it would stand to reason they have you use John's name. How do you feel about it?"

"On the one hand, I'm happy that my father wouldn't give me up for adoption to John. On the other hand, I feel even more confused as to why my mother and stepfather chose to keep this information from me for so long. I've been an adult for a couple of years now. Most of my girlfriends from school are already married, and half of them are with child or have one. Why couldn't they see me as an adult?"

"Because they are parents, and parents never quite see their children as adults. I received my first inkling of that the other day from my father. He treated and spoke to me as if I were an adult for the first time ever, a truly wonderful and unique experience. However, I am twenty-three, I lived on my own for four years and have run the plantation for two."

"You are probably right." She sighed and reclined against the back of the bench seat.

"I have seen it with my mother and grandmother, as well," he continued. "When my grandmother arrives for an extended visit, she treats my mother like she is still a child, instructing her in the best way to do this or that. It is not as though my mother does not already know how to run a household. She's been doing that for twenty-five years. Even so, Grandmother feels this need to instruct her grown children. Mother tends to be patient about it, but I have seen her roll her eyes heavenward a few times."

Holly chuckled. "My grandmother is much the same. My mother, however, was a bit more outspoken than yours."

"Your mother? No, that is not possible." Bryce chuckled.

Holly swatted him on the shoulder.

"And I know who will be the same."

The joyful moment melted away. "I'll never have those moments with my mother, will I?"

Bryce reached over and placed his hand over hers. "No, I suppose you will not. I am sorry."

Fresh tears welled in her eyes as grief bubbled to the surface. She glanced away and looked at the Savannah River. She pictured herself on a gondola floating down its silver current, away from the pain and into the unknown.

Chapter 6

Holly clutched the bundle of letters. All were addressed via Lloyd Jarvis. She noted the dates they were received, which spanned years. She understood Bryce's father's legal responsibility not to give them to her until the appointed time, but she still wished he had broken protocol. Holly's mind and arms were full as she and Bryce headed down toward the river and west of the city to the spot where his friend said he docked.

"Ahoy, Henry!" Bryce called out.

A man looking very dapper in his sailor blues and white shirt popped his head out of the makeshift cabin. "You came. I didn't expect to see you. Is this the damsel in distress?" He stepped from the boat to the dock with the confident stride that came from one familiar with working on the water.

"Henry, this is my good friend Holly Landers. Holly,

this is Henry Rushton, a bit of a scallywag and scoundrel." Bryce winked at Holly.

It seemed odd to hear Bryce use her real last name, and yet it felt right. "It is a pleasure to meet you, Mr. Rushton."

"Call me Henry. Everyone does. Besides, I don't cotton to the Southern formalities. Well, not all of them. I do know how to treat a lady, however. May I assist you and invite you to a tour of my boat, Miss Landers?"

She took his proffered hand and stepped down from the buggy. Bryce found his place right beside her. *He's protective.* Holly noted to keep this smooth talker at arm's length. "I would be honored to investigate your fine vessel, Mr. Rushton."

"Henry, please. Come on, Bryce, give the little woman the freedom."

"It is her choice. Holly has always had a mind of her own."

"Ah, I do believe you've told me that in the past. You, however, neglected to tell me how beautiful this woman is. If you had, I would have come much sooner and swept her away from you."

Bryce narrowed his gaze on Henry.

"Are you being courted, Miss Landers?" Henry asked. "If not, I should like to put my name in with your father. After the proper time of mourning has been completed, of course."

Holly looked down at her hands.

"She is spoken for, Henry."

"I suppose the better man, huh, Bryce? I would only take you on wild adventures and tour the world for unknown countries and peoples." Henry kissed the top of her hand and released her.

Holly's face flushed. Bryce wrapped a protective arm

around her shoulders. "Turn down the charm, Henry. Holly has been through quite enough the past few days."

"I am sorry, Miss Landers. No harm intended. Please forgive my foolishness. I am sorry for your loss."

Holly nodded, unable to speak. Her emotions churned within like an eddy on the edge of the river swirling down into an unseen pit. She felt trapped, spinning out of control. She closed her eyes for balance. A tear released. Bryce took out a soft handkerchief and wiped it away.

"I really am sorry, Miss Landers." Henry's voice lost all its bravado.

"You are forgiven, Henry."

He smiled. "Well, then, since I made such a fool of myself, perhaps the tour will help absolve my blunder."

They followed him onto his boat and into the cabin. The small engine at the stern would propel the boat up-river. The rudder, he explained, needed to be enlarged for greater control. The inside of the cabin appeared clean, neat and practical.

"You see, I have a bed, a table there that pulls up from the wall, a chair, plus a barrel for additional seating. The cabinet over here has all my food supplies, and my clothing is under the bed." He lifted the mattress and revealed the convenient storage space. "The boat had more leaks than I could find so I tarred the hull over and over again. She's holding her own now. And I have a small stove for cooking and heating. All the comforts of home."

"You did a fine job, Henry." Bryce continued to scan the homey cabin.

"I love the bluish-lilac color of the walls," Holly offered.

"Thank you. I mixed a couple of leftover cans of paint and had enough to do the interior."

"What are you doing for work these days, Henry?" Bryce asked.

"Have a seat." Henry motioned Holly to the chair, Bryce to the barrel, and he sat on the bed. "Working for Father, on the plantation. I've been trying to implement some of the new planting policies we were taught in school. Father won't have a thing to do with modern, though."

"I am at an advantage there. My father has let me do all that I would like with the plantation."

"Is he still upset that you didn't become a lawyer?"

"No. He has agreed I run a plantation better than I would have done as an attorney."

"I am considering traveling the world for a spell. Father says I am not thinking straight. But when else can a man travel except for when he is unencumbered?" Henry gave half a nod in Holly's direction.

"Holly and I are hoping to go to Europe," Bryce said. Holly glanced over at him. Just how much had he planned on the two of them becoming a couple and marriage?

"Yes, if it wasn't for you and all the tales you told in college, I do not believe I'd have these traveling notions."

Holly gasped. "You spoke of our…"

Bryce saw the horror in her eyes that he might have betrayed a confidence. "I simply told him of the places we read about and that both of us would like to travel there one day." His firm gaze sent a bold message, assuring her he would not break the confidence of their romantic childhood notions of being a king and queen and traveling the land as knights, or as Robin Hood and Maid Marion, or other fanciful adventurers.

Henry's boisterous laugh broke the intense, silent conversation between Holly and Bryce. "I would love to hear those stories."

Holly shot him a penetrating glare.

"Or maybe I would not." Henry stood. "Would you two

like to join me for supper this evening or do you have other plans?"

"It is up to Holly."

"It is a kind offer and would probably be most entertaining. I'm not sure I am ready to hear about Bryce and his college years. You make him sound a bit of a rogue."

"Ah, but, Miss Landers, he was. He left many a girl's heart broken when he would not get serious and date more than once."

"Henry, you have a loose tongue," Bryce chided.

"Only because I love seeing you squirm. So, will you join me this evening?"

Holly got up and slipped her hand in the crook of Bryce's elbow. "Not tonight. But will you do us the honor of coming to my home tomorrow night? You can tell me then all the tales of your college adventures with Bryce."

Bryce placed his hand on top of hers. "Not all of our tales." Bryce gave Henry directions to Holly's house.

They left the boat and settled back in the buggy before Holly spoke. "He is a bit untamed."

Bryce laughed. "Yes, he is. I am afraid he helped me get into trouble I would not have done on my own. But it was not his fault. I chose to partake in the folly on more than one occasion."

"This is a side of you I have never seen."

"Of course you have. It is no different than the time we went out shrimping and 'borrowed' a boat. Unfortunately, Mr. Silvers did not see it as playful borrowing. I could not sit down for a week."

Holly giggled. "I didn't get in trouble for that one."

"Because I took full responsibility. My father never told your parents. I think in part because they were embarrassed that their son would stoop so low as to steal a boat."

"Yeah, but I was the one who suggested it."

"Father did not know that." Bryce smiled.

"I also turned down Henry's dinner invitation in order for us to have time to read all these letters." She glanced down at the stack. "Perhaps not all. There are a lot here."

"It appears your father meant what he said about you always being a part of his thoughts."

"It is reassuring but…" She let her words trail off. The horse's hooves on the ballast-stone road clicked with a certain rhythm that mirrored the gentle rock of the carriage.

"I have just the place. Let me swing by a store and then I will take you…"

She glanced at him. "What?"

He closed his eyes then quickly glanced at the road and back again to Holly. "Last night I opened my mouth and blundered by suggesting you and I go to Venice as man and wife."

She placed her fingers over his lips. They were warm and soft. Desire welled up inside her. "I understand." She removed her fingers and looked away. "I have a confession to make. For years I longed for you and me to…to… be more than playmates, than childhood friends grown up. All those letters we shared while you were in college. It seemed like we were getting closer. And then you came back and…nothing. You pulled away. So I buried my feelings."

"Holly, I am so sorry. I felt we were getting closer, as well. Your father would not allow me to court you until you were twenty-one. I struggled with my desires and my need to respect your father and his wishes. So I pulled away. My heart never left, but I could not tell you my heart's intentions without compromising your father's expressed desire that I not pursue you. I do love you, Holly. I always have. Although I admit I did not realize the depth of my love for you until I was away at college."

Holly blushed at his brazen declaration. "Then why all the women at college that Henry mentioned? You certainly did not tell me about those in your letters."

A red glow grew from the base of his neck up to his ears and flushed his cheeks. "No, I did not tell you. And Henry made me sound more of a rogue than I truly was. Yes, I did take several women out to various social functions at the school. I promise you that I provided nothing more than an escort. It seemed the right thing to do at the time. You were still in school and, well, we had not expressed our feelings toward one another."

"So why only one date with each woman?"

"If there was no friendship like the one I enjoyed with you, why pursue a relationship? And in your letters I found a peace, a connection with you."

Holly fought off the jumbled words playing across her mind. She wanted to know more. Today seemed inappropriate to have such an intimate conversation. "Bryce, I am unsettled by this line of discussion."

Bryce allowed a brief silence to hang between them. "I have a place where we can read those letters in private. However, before I take you there I want you to understand my reasoning."

"And the reasoning is?"

Bryce watched the road in front of them for a moment then looked back at Holly. "I own my own house. It is a small place. I was hoping it would become our home. I have a lot of work to do on it still, but I am happy with how it is progressing."

"Your own house? But you are still living with your parents."

"My parents don't know about the house. Father would have told me to invest the money. Mother would have... Well, I am not sure how Mother would have reacted. I just know I wanted to keep it private, for us. Holly, I am an honorable man. I have never, nor would I ever, dishonor a woman. I love you and want you to be my wife. I should not be telling you all of this at this point in time. You are the only person I am unable to keep my deepest and most intimate thoughts from."

Holly couldn't believe her ears. "Didn't you just a few hours ago refuse to enter my bedroom for fear of wagging tongues? Now you are suggesting I go to a house where no one else is and be alone with you, a house that you apparently plan on being our home? And you want me to go unchaperoned?"

Bryce groaned. "What was I thinking? Forgive me, please."

Holly chuckled and placed her hand on his. "You know me too well. You know I am not overly concerned about social pretexts because I know God knows how I behave or don't behave. I would love to see your house. But I know I am vulnerable right now, and being alone with you at this point in time could be a temptation I am not ready to handle."

"Ah. So does that mean there is hope for you and me?"

Holly eased out a pent-up breath. "Yes, there is hope. And I really want to see this house. Where did you get the money?"

"Grandfather left me an inheritance, which I invested, and I have also been saving as much as possible. Father paid for my college education so I had no expenses there, and you know I worked every semester, so I just kept saving and investing. I found the place last year. The original owners had neglected it for years. I managed to purchase it at quite a reasonable price. I can show it to you. I will stay outside and you can see the inside."

"I would like that."

"There is a garden in the side and backyard. I am hoping to plant lots of flowers. That will be a part of the finishing touches. For now, I am concentrating on the buildings themselves. It is a small two-story home with a detached carriage house. Above the carriage house is an additional room for guests or boarders. I am going to make a closed-in entryway from the carriage house to the main house in the event of bad weather. I think you will like it, Holly."

"I think I will." Holly shifted in her seat.

"Perhaps we can sit in the backyard and read the letters. It will be private but exposed."

"That will be fine."

"Wonderful. I shall run into the market and get us something to eat."

Holly agreed.

While Bryce retreated into the store she opened the letter her father had given her mother for his little girl. That was fifteen years ago.

My Sweet Pumpkin,

I honestly don't know where to begin this letter. So many thoughts are swimming in my brain, and yet I don't know what to write. I love you, and I hope you will forgive me for stepping aside and letting John Graham raise you. I saw no good coming out of confusing a young child who had such a rough time growing up without a father for so many years.

My heart aches leaving you behind but I know I'm doing right by you. You are a precious gift from God, one of which I was unworthy. I have a confession. I sent your mother and you back to her parents because I had gotten myself into some trouble at the beginning of the war. I chose to fight for the North, even though all my neighbors chose to fight for the

South. Your mother was unaware of my decision, and perhaps that is why news came back to her that I had died in battle, when in fact, I had not.

I was a bit wild in my youth. War changed me. Seeing your mother in love with another man, anguished all over again over the loss of her first love, also had a profound effect. I have rededicated my life to God and will be doing my best to live a life more worthy of Him.

I did not share all of this with your mother because her decision was already difficult. By law, your mother was still married to me. However, in her heart she was more in love with John Graham. She had loved me, but had mourned my death and buried that love years hence.

As for you, your mother said you had a difficult time accepting John as your father. They had been married six months before you called him "Daddy." Two months later, I returned. But I couldn't bear to hurt you. So I returned to my home, the home your mother and I worked hard to build, and even harder to keep in my family. The original homestead belonged to my grandfather. He'd given it to me for our wedding present. I was a teacher then, and the small community needed a teacher. But teachers aren't paid much so your mother and I worked hard to have the homestead become self-sufficient. Then news hit about the war.

I saw the house before traveling here. It suffered a lot of damage during the war. But the bones are strong and I can rebuild. Someday I hope you will want to come and see the place of your birth. I would love to show it to you.

For now, know that I love you. I will always love

you. And I told your mother if she ever needed my help I would come.

Forgive me for releasing you into the care of your mother and John Graham, but my home is not a place for a young child at this time.

All my love,

Daddy

Bryce watched Holly as he approached the carriage. He loaded the small bundle behind the seat and climbed up inside the buggy. Fresh tears streamed down her face as she looked up from the paper in front of her.

"Which letter?"

"The first. The one he left with my mother." She sniffed.

He handed her a clean handkerchief. Perhaps he should have brought more than three. "How do you feel?"

"I can tell that he loved me. And he's confessing to me things he never confessed to Momma, which is rather strange."

"What kinds of things?"

"Apparently he fought for the North."

"Oh. And he is from Tennessee?"

She nodded. "And if I remember my history on the War Between the States, Tennessee was the location for a lot of the battles."

"Yes, it was."

Bryce grabbed the reins and led the buggy into the wide Savannah streets. "What else did he say?"

"That he had gotten himself into some trouble before the war. Perhaps it had a bit to do with his politics at the time."

"Yeah, it would not have been a safe place to live if he sided with the North."

"He and Mother would have had some interesting discussions regarding the war, if they had stayed together. Grandpa had his share of slaves."

"As did mine. I see both sides, but I agree no man should own another." He worked his way south toward his house. "My house is only a few blocks from Forsythe Park."

Holly slipped the letter back into the envelope. "I never saw your father as overbearing. I am having trouble trying to understand why you would keep the purchase of your home from him."

"He is not overbearing?" Bryce rubbed the back of his neck. "Do you recall what happened when I defied Father and changed my major to business instead of law?"

"He wasn't pleased."

"Perhaps that is all you saw, but I had to go through weeks of long letters, a summer of constant questions and debates on the merits of law over the merits of business. Fortunately for me, debating classes were ones I excelled in. He does not like change, and once he sets his mind on how something should be, it takes an army to sway him in another direction, or in my case, years. I simply did not have time for the arguments if I were to improve the property in a timely manner. You do turn twenty-one in a few months."

"Ah." Holly looked away.

"Holly, have I upset you?"

Holly sighed. "Bryce, I know you mean well. But this talk of marriage and courting…it is a little overwhelming." She paused. "It is not just that Momma died, although that is there. My biggest problem is the manipulation of my life. First my mother and father decide not to tell me who I really am. My real father leaves me without consulting me. Of course, I was only five, but I still feel as though I should have had some say. Now you are bringing me to a home you planned to present me with after we start to court. And your intention is to marry me. It is just too much. I know I said there was hope for a future. But right now I cannot take the added stress, or for that matter, someone else telling me what I should and should not do."

Bryce's back stiffened and waited for further blows. He had told his mother he'd wait, and what had he done? Invited Holly to his home. "Forgive me, Holly."

"I think if the issues of Mother dying and my having another father had never come up, I wouldn't have a problem with this. But I am different now. I have little patience for people telling me what to do. I am sorry, Bryce. Would you please take me home? I cannot do this right now."

Chapter 7

Bryce didn't say another word on the way home, which Holly appreciated. Once home, she excused herself from dinner, ran up to her room and set about reading her father's letters. After the third, she tucked them back in their envelopes and retied them together. She felt she finally understood her father's love and rationale. He was not without blame, to be sure, but he seemed as much of a victim as she. They needed to talk.

A gentle knock at the door startled her. "Holly?"

"Not now, Bryce."

"Holly, please."

She went to the door and opened it. She gave him the look she knew he'd understand from years of growing up together.

"I have failed you. I am sorry. I only wanted to give you a secure place where we could have some privacy reading the letters. I should not have suggested going to my house at all."

"Bryce, I know you didn't mean any harm by it. I am uncertain about everything."

"I know. And I am sorry. I will not suggest marriage, courting, kissing, anything of the sort again, I promise."

Holly relaxed her posture. "Give me time, Bryce."

"Call when you wish to speak with me. I shall not impose myself upon you again." Bryce stepped back.

She wanted to pull him back and tell him that wasn't what she meant. But she had meant it. She still meant it. She needed space from him, from her stepfather and possibly even from her father. "Goodbye, Bryce."

He nodded and silently made his way to the stairs.

At the same time, Emmett Landers came down the hall. "May I have a word with you, Holly?" he asked.

"Yes, come in." She stepped back and held the door open for him.

He glanced at the bundle of letters on the bed. "I am glad you received them. I fear my presence is causing you further anxiety, so I have decided I should return home at first light."

"Please, sit. I do have some questions for you."

He sat on the chair and she on the bed. "First, I understand why you chose what you did. I just do not understand the reasons for keeping me in the dark so long. Who decided on twenty-one?"

"Your mother. I agreed."

"So, John and Mother decided first."

"I do not know what John's discussions with your mother were. I only know she suggested it. I thought twenty-one was a bit old, but she convinced me you would need to be strong enough to handle this information."

"I do not feel strong."

"Honey, I understand the hurt you are feeling. And I hate to say the phrase 'we thought we were doing what was right for you' again, but…"

"I know, it fits."

"What happened between you and Mr. Jarvis today? If you do not mind me asking?"

"He has wanted to court me for a several years now. My father John had asked him to wait until I was twenty-one. Lord knows how many other men may have come for permission to court me and were told the same. Honestly, if Momma hadn't died, I would love to be courted by Bryce. He and I have a friendship that is different from any other person I know. But I am not in a mood to be manipulated."

"How was he manipulating you?"

"He was not…exactly. I just felt that my life was being settled without my knowledge. I know many young women would take no issue with that. But I am different. He has purchased a house for us already."

Emmett Landers raised his eyebrows and sat back in his chair. "He is a confident young man."

"And then some. He is a good man. But recent events have proved that I have been lied to most of my life. Others have decided who I should be, what I should do and when I should do it, and I will not lead a life like that any longer. Not after Momma died. I wish she were here so I could ask her some questions."

"You mean, so you could argue with her and passionately dig for the answers you are searching for."

Holly smiled. "You knew her well. Which means, I guess you know me some."

"Some. Let me tell you a little secret. Your mother and I had some pretty intense arguments. I have my own stubborn streak, so you might just have even a tad more than your mother's trait in there."

"I read Momma's letter. But she wrote that without knowing how I would react. She wrote it as a 'just in case' letter. I cannot talk to her about it, cannot ask so many questions I have that only she can answer. It's not fair."

"No, darlin', it isn't fair. So what questions can I answer for you? And, trust me, you can speak in whatever volume and intensity you feel toward me. I am not afraid of your frustration."

Holly giggled. "You might just regret having said that."

"No, I won't. But take note. I do not mind passion, but I will not tolerate speaking ill of your mother. Me, I can take it because I am here to defend myself, if need be. Your mother, however, is not here, and I still love and respect her. She had to make some hard choices over the years."

Holly looked at the stranger sitting across from her, a man of impeccable honor and grace. She could see why her mother had fallen in love with him as a girl. "First question. Where did you and Momma meet?"

They spoke until midnight. They spoke until Holly felt her mind growing numb, saturated with information that would need to be digested.

"I really must get to sleep," Emmett said with a yawn. "The morning train leaves at dawn."

"Can't you stay another day, Daddy?"

He beamed, stood and walked over to her. He kissed the top of her head. "I must depart tomorrow. But for you I shall leave on the last train. We will go into the city and you can show me all your favorite places."

"I would like that."

"Bryce Jarvis, what did you do to her?" John Graham slammed the front door behind him, confronting Bryce on the veranda. "She is barely talking to me and she went to her room without dinner last night. What happened?"

"It is hard to say. She is feeling manipulated, and I did not help put the fire out on those feelings."

"What did you do?"

"Expressed my feelings for her."

The clench of John Graham's jaw said it all. "I told you to wait until she was twenty-one."

"And that is part of her problem. You decided for her to not be told about her real identity until she was twenty-one. You decided for her not to be allowed to court until she was twenty-one. And now most of her friends are already married and with children. You have made her a recluse in her own town. And for what purpose? How many suitors did you tell to wait until she was twenty-one?"

John turned his back on Bryce and stormed back into the house.

Bryce finished up his work at the Grahams' home and headed back to his own place. He'd left his house unattended since the accident. Bryce resolved to finish his house, put it on the market and get on with his life. His dreams with Holly were lost. He understood how she felt manipulated, even though that had not been his intent. Even if they did have a slim chance of a future together, he couldn't see them living in this house. Not now.

He found the house in the same state he'd left it in a week before. All the special-ordered cabinets were in the middle of the kitchen floor. He should have had the carpenter put them in, but he'd thought he'd save a few dollars and install them himself. All the details that had made his heart leap just a few days hence now weighed heavily upon him. The joy of making this house ready for Holly had left him. Bryce put down his tools and went to the cabinetmaker's shop. He left with a date for the installation of the cabinets. Then he secured another craftsman to finish the floors the next week. He went back to the house and piled up the debris into his wagon.

Exhausted after completing two hours of grueling work and a couple of dump runs, he unhitched the horse from his wagon, saddled the equally tired animal and headed toward his parents' home. He had a date for the cabinet installation, another for finishing the floors. Tomorrow he'd secure someone to paint and wallpaper. In a couple of weeks he could put the house on the market. He knew he'd make a profit. But he had wanted a home, a special place where he and Holly could begin a life together. He hoped they still had a chance but...

"Is that you, Bryce?" his mother called from the kitchen.

"Yes, ma'am."

"Where have you been? John is fit to be tied. I have never seen him so upset. What happened between you and Holly yesterday?"

"He is not upset with what happened between Holly and me. I suppose he could be, but he is really upset because I pointed out that if he had not waited until Holly was twenty-one she would not be suffering so. I am certain she had many a gentleman wanting to court her, and they probably got the same rejection I did. I never realized how controlling he was."

"That may be so, but something did happen between you and Holly, and I want to know what that was."

"Trust me, Mother. I shall fix it. Holly just needs time."

"No, that won't do. Tell me what happened, Bryce. All of my female instincts are saying you declared your love to her and she rejected it."

"Something like that."

"Why are you keeping this such a secret?"

"Because it is my secret, not yours, not Father's. I made

a mistake and I am paying for it. I will deal with it in my own way. Please do not push this matter, Mother."

"Very well, I will back away. But I am certain your father will want specifics. John says Holly is leaving on the six o'clock train with Emmett Landers."

"She is going to Tennessee?"

"Apparently. You see why I am asking what happened?"

"Yes, but…" He glanced at his watch then ran out to the barn. With any luck he could get to the station before the train left.

"Holly, please do not leave," John Graham pleaded.

"Father, I told you, I will return. I feel the best place for me right now is with the Landers family. Tiffany can help around the house while I am gone. And please do not worry about propriety—half this town likely knows that Emmett is my father."

John stepped back and released his hold on Holly. "I love you."

"I love you, too." She wiped a tear from her eye. "I will return soon. I promise."

Holly accepted Emmett's hand and stepped up into the buggy. "I will take good care of our girl, John."

"I know you will, Emmett."

Emmett climbed up onto the wagon and headed for the train station. "Are you certain now is the time you want to come to Tennessee?"

"Yes. I think it will be easier if I go. People there do not know me. They won't be making plans for my life without my say-so."

Emmett smiled. "I cannot guarantee that I won't act like a father and tell you what I think is best. Especially once you are under my roof."

"Fathers can be overbearing." She giggled.

"But they are not who you are running from right now. It is a certain young man who…"

"Who has fallen into the same trap as John Graham. Apparently there have been several others who asked permission to court me. Bryce is the only one who stayed unattached, according to Father."

"Tell me, why do you call John by the formal use of 'Father'?"

Holly leaned back in the bench seat. "I don't know. I have always called him 'Father.'"

"No, when you were five you called him 'Daddy.' I remember that."

"I suppose maybe I did. I don't remember when I started calling him 'Father.' But it has been a long time, goes back to some of my earliest memories."

"And yet you call me 'Dad' and 'Daddy.'"

"It seems natural to call you that."

"But not John?"

"The other children call him 'Papa.' For some reason I always thought of John as Father, not Papa." They were nearing other carriages parked at the train station. One of the boys would come by later and pick up the horse and buggy. They climbed down to the dusty road and Emmett gathered their bags. Holly took her smaller bag that carried her purse and a few items to freshen up with while en route.

"Holly" she heard. She'd know that voice anywhere. She turned to see Bryce's horse come to a thundering stop from a full gallop. A brown cloud thick with road grit swirled around them all. Bryce jumped off the horse and walked quickly to face her.

"Bryce?" She coughed and waved the dirt away from her eyes and nose. "What are you doing here?"

"Mother said you were going to Tennessee with your father."

"I am." She bolstered her resolve, standing erect to her full height of five feet five inches, still quite less than Bryce's six feet.

"Please do not leave because of me. I shall stay away. I won't put any undue burden on you."

"Bryce," she cried, "you don't understand. It is not you as much as it is me. Going to Tennessee allows me a chance to get to know my dad better as well as meet my other siblings. No one knows who I am out there. I won't be wondering if so-and-so knows, or if everyone is laughing behind my back because I was ignorant that I was not John Graham's real daughter. It will also allow me a chance to get used to my real name. Don't you see? I am doing this for me."

She watched as his face contorted in a way she had never witnessed before. Then the twitching muscles quickly settled into a tight-lipped, clenched set of the jaw that she most definitely understood. His back became rifle-straight and just as immovable.

As Holly watched, Bryce stuffed a tornado of emotions he didn't know how to handle into a box and clamped the lid down tight. The words that escaped from those pursed lips came out in a monotone of non-emotion. "Fine," he said flatly. No anger. No tenderness. That one word could have been a saddlebag falling to the ground for all its lack of expression. "Whatever you decide is fine by me. Please, know that I…"

Holly took the few steps that separated them and leaned against the sweaty, heaving side of Bryce's horse. She reached up and touched Bryce's cheek. "I know," she said in a soothing voice, "and I care for you, too. Just give me time, please."

Bryce released a long, slow breath. "Let me help you to the train." She saw the kindness in his eyes and allowed herself a smile. He took the bag from her hand and escorted them to the train station.

Emmett placed his bags down and ordered their tickets.

Holly wanted to do so many things. She wanted to call out her forgiveness. But she didn't want to cause a scene in public. They were already attracting curious stares. Instead, she opted to place her hand on top of his. She glanced into his honey-brown eyes and waited for a response. They lit with hope. "Call on me when you return, Holly."

"I shall."

He waited on the platform until the train pulled away, and she watched him slowly fade into the backdrop of the station and disappear.

"Are you certain this is what you want to do, daughter?"

"Yes, Daddy, I am sure." Holly's voice quivered.

As the train pulled out and rocked back and forth on the rails, Holly saw the Savannah River pulling away. The life she once knew departed quickly, just like the river. The rocking, the racket and the drift of the Savannah from her view held no resemblance to the gentle drift of an imaginary gondola down the canals of Venice. Why run from Bryce when all they had ever been to one another was each other's best friend? Holly closed her eyes and tried to hold back the tears. She was running. The very thing that Bryce had tried to help her avoid.

"Do you want to talk about it, darlin'?"

A fortnight had passed with no word from Holly. Bryce's relationship with John Graham had diminished to the point that Bryce no longer helped the Grahams and stayed away when their mutual families got together. It was evident that John blamed Bryce for Holly's departure and Bryce couldn't fault the man for his opinion because he agreed—at least to a point.

He stood in the house that no longer gave him joy, as beautiful as it had become. The cabinets were in. The floors were refinished and looked like new. The painter had begun putting up the wallpaper in the dining room and front parlor. Bryce worked on the exterior, and even though Holly was gone, he continued with his father's schedule of having his brothers, Chad and Ryan, run the plantation. He spent most of his time at the house.

He scanned the house once again. Next week it would be ready to sell. All of his plans and dreams would be for someone else. Hopefully that someone would have a good life in this house, the kind he'd been hoping and praying for with Holly.

"Hello?" a familiar female voice called from the front door.

"Catherine? What are you doing here?"

His sister came into view with her slightly protruding belly. "I had Michael follow you yesterday and report where you've been going every day. So, who owns this place?"

"I do. I'm about to put it on the market."

"May I have a look around?"

"Of course." Bryce escorted his sister through the various rooms and concluded with the kitchen.

"This is very nice. You've put a lot of work into it."

If only he had kept his secret a little longer. Perhaps Holly wouldn't feel so hedged in. "Thank you."

"You bought this for Holly, didn't you?"

"It was foolish, I know, but yes, I did. Little did I know that her mother would pass away and…"

"Her life would be turned upside down," Catherine finished for him. "How is she doing?"

"Haven't heard from her since she went to Tennessee."

"Oh, so you don't know she returned on last evening's train."

"No, I did not." Bryce scanned the room for a possible place to sit. Seeing nothing he asked, "Would you like to sit in the garden? There is still much to do, but there are several benches where we can rest."

"That would be nice. I came to talk with you about the problems between you and the Grahams."

"There is nothing to say. John Graham blames me for pushing Holly away. I cannot blame him. If I hadn't…"

"What did you do?"

He took hold of his sister's elbow and escorted her to the backyard and to one of the benches that sat under a tall magnolia tree. "Nothing disrespectful. However, it was not the time to share with Holly my plans and hopes for the future. I knew better. Holly is Holly, and she has a mind and will of her own. What was I thinking that this grand surprise would be a welcomed gift to her? Instead it was an albatross that sunk her into a further pit of confusion. The real problem is, she came to me to help her navigate through these emotions, and what did I do? I put further complications into her life. I am such a fool. She will never want or trust me again."

"Time will help."

"Perhaps. But I do not give it much hope."

"How are you going to mend the fence with John Graham?"

"I do not believe I can. I know details about the past that he is not comfortable with my knowing." He looked up at the house. "Perhaps I should move into this house, then maybe Mom and Dad can maintain their close relationship with the Grahams."

"What about work on the plantation?"

"Father gave me three months' leave, so I decided I would take it. I'm hoping to profit from the sale of the house. I will buy another and refurbish it like I did this one."

"Bryce." She placed a hand on his forearm. "I know you are hurting right now. But don't give up on Holly. Give her the time she needs."

"I have decided I will wait until the end of the year. If she does not contact me by then, I shall assume she is not interested. Until then, I will keep to myself, do the work needed for the family plantation and anything else."

"Perhaps living on your own might give you and both families the space they need. Can I help you move in?"

Bryce chuckled. "I haven't even told Mom and Dad about this place yet."

"Ah, well, Michael told me in front of them."

"Seems like I am making bad choices in all sorts of directions. What did Father say?"

"Nothing. He seemed perplexed. But he does have the address, so don't be surprised if he stops by."

"Thank you for the warning." He glanced into his sister's eyes. "I need time to heal, as well, I guess. Thanks for your caring, and for being a treasured member of my family. Speaking of which, when will this niece or nephew be making an appearance?"

"In mid-February, we hope."

"I am happy for you."

Moving into the house suddenly seemed the logical choice. He knew his mother and father would find it odd, but they would support him and his decisions.

Holly sat at the Jarvises' dinner table, surprised to find Bryce absent for the evening. To find he had moved to town into his own house sent an uneasy vibration in her spine. She missed him in so many ways, but when she heard mention of the house, the knot in her stomach tightened again.

She'd been home for three days and life had gradually settled into place. The Grahams were all still grieving, but normalcy prevailed. Holly took care of the household and the younger children. Her father had gone back to work while she'd visited her Tennessee family.

Tennessee… She could still picture everyone's face. Daddy had been right; the family accepted her as if she'd always been one of them. And in fact, she had been. Emmett Landers had never hidden the fact that he'd been married once before and that he had a daughter from that marriage.

He had helped her deal with her grief for her mother, encouraging her to cry, be angry and do whatever it took to get rid of the bottled emotions that came with the loss of a loved one. She liked Emmett and had grown to love him. And she knew that he loved her. But she knew her place was here in Savannah, helping her family deal with the loss. She loved them, and she had missed them.

She had the most concern for Tiffany. She seemed to be attracted to the bad boys in school; the ones who pulled practical jokes, who didn't study, who seemed to live life on the edge. She had even smelled some alcohol on her breath one day.

Holly's relationship with her stepfather had changed. He became overly protective. He feared Emmett's influence in her life. In truth, he seemed fearful he would lose her. He blamed Bryce for her sudden departure and no amount of persuasion could convince him otherwise. His part—his responsibility—in the decades-long subterfuge did not register in his mind.

"Holly, can you pass the bread, please?" Tiff asked.

She reached for the pewter platter and handed it to the person on her left and watched the platter make its rounds until it made its destination in front of Tiffany.

"Thank you."

It felt so odd not seeing Bryce at the table.

"John, how are you doing?" Mrs. Jarvis asked.

"Regaining some of the normalcy back in my life—our lives." He scanned the table and lingered on Holly for a moment longer than the rest. He was hurt. She knew he didn't understand the betrayal she felt. And she knew he was happy to see her home.

"And how are you young folk doing in school?"

"I miss Mommy," Calvin said, pouting. "I miss Bryce, too. Where is he?"

"He lives in his own home now, sweetheart," Cynthia Jarvis explained. She ran her fingers through Calvin's red hair, a connection Holly had with him.

"We don't live here and we came for supper."

Lloyd chuckled. "That is true, son. But Bryce is a man now and is making his own home. Which means he has all kinds of chores he has to do on his own."

Holly tensed. Was Lloyd Jarvis implying she should be in that home with Bryce? "Personally, I think he should have saved his money. But then again, he has a good mind for business. He purchased the house at a great price, and even with all that he spent on improvements he stands to make a nice profit. In fact, he's looking to purchase another home and do the same after this one sells."

"A man ought not to invest in too many homes." John's words soured the atmosphere in the room.

"He is selling?" Holly blurted. "But he was so excited about that house and all the improvements he was making."

Mrs. Jarvis stood. "He is a wise man. I know he shall

do well for himself. Can I bring out some blueberry pie for anyone?"

The table conversation dissolved into the energetic cheers of all the younger children. Holly knew that she would have to have another conversation with her stepfather. He needed to understand she'd left for Tennessee because of the confusion he and her mother had introduced into her life…not Bryce.

The rest of the evening dragged for Holly. She no longer seemed to fit as she once had. Bryce had always been her companion, as well as Catherine.

After they arrived home and she'd seen the younger children to bed, she approached John's office and tapped the door frame. "Father?"

"Yes." He lifted his head. A sea of paperwork was scattered around the table.

"May I have a word with you?"

"Of course, you know I am always here for you."

She smiled. "Yes, I know, Father. I am concerned by your apparent distrust or dislike for Bryce. He did nothing wrong."

"If he hadn't…"

"He did nothing wrong. He simply assumed I would court him once you gave us permission. His assumption felt controlling. Forgive me, but it is the very same issue I am having with you and Mother."

"We never meant to control you."

"I know that. Emmett helped me to understand. However, that does not take away from the fact that I have had suitors and you had not informed me. In fact, you turned them all away, just like Bryce. Why didn't you allow me to have the potential of marrying a man before I turned twenty-one?"

John Graham paled.

"This is why I left. I needed time to clear my head. I needed space from the pain of losing Momma, and the pain of not knowing my father. He is a good man."

"Honey, I know he is a good man. That wasn't the point."

"No, deceit was. I am not a Graham. I am a Landers, and yet you had me believe I was a Graham all of my life. Why not tell me the truth? Even at eight I would have understood."

John pursed his lips. "I can see how you might view it that way. There were other reasons for my decisions. I will simply leave it at that."

"Fine, I will not push you for more details. I love you, Father. I always will. But don't try to hold on to me too tightly. I would more than likely be inclined to rebel."

"Ah, your mother warned me about that. I shall try."

"Father, I am taking control over my own life. From now on I will allow men to come to you for possibly courting me, but you will speak to me and I will decide. Am I making myself clear on this point?"

John stiffened. "Quite. This is not how I raised you."

"No, it is not. But suffice it to say there are some losses that have come into our lives that go beyond the loss of Mother."

John nodded.

She leaned into him and gave him a kiss on the cheek. "I still love you."

"And I you, daughter."

She smiled and noticed the slight wrinkles around her father's eyes. "Good night, Father. I will see you in the morning."

If only she had the right words to say to Bryce.

Chapter 8

Today marked the two-month anniversary of her mother's death, and the loss had taken its toll on the family. Holly's concerns focused on her siblings. Tiffany seemed more distant. She'd been staying later and later after school. Holly prayed daily for Tiff.

She set the table for dinner. Tiffany should be home soon. The boys had arrived an hour ago. *Please, Lord, keep her safe,* she prayed in silence.

The heavy thud of a door meeting its jambs and the scuffle of approaching boots on the hardwood floor broke the solitude of her kitchen sanctuary.

"Where's Tiff?" Calvin said as he plopped a rabbit on the counter.

"Take that outside and prepare it, young man. You know better."

"You're mean. Momma would have helped me."

"Momma would have tanned your hide for bringing it

in here, and you know that. Now take it outside and start preparing it." The boys knew better than to kill an animal if they weren't going to eat it. Holly didn't care for rabbit stew but Calvin loved it. The only time she served it was after he hunted one down.

The front door slammed open. Holly turned to see Tiffany running through the great room toward the stairs. "Calvin, take that out of here and then wash up." She removed all the pans from the hot surface of the stove and wiped her hands on the white apron around her waist.

Holly hurried from the kitchen, hitched up her skirt to run up the stairs and followed after Tiffany. She stopped at the bedroom and gave a gentle knock on the painted panel door. "Tiff?" Muted cries were the only response. She turned the fluted glass knob and opened the door. Tiffany lay sprawled across the bed, crying into her pillow.

"Honey, what is the matter?"

Tiffany didn't respond. Her stifled cries increased to wailing.

Holly sat beside her on the bed. "What happened?"

"Nothing," she murmured.

"Is it Momma?"

Tiffany's chocolate swirls tossed back and forth. "Maybe a little. Mostly it was Bobby. He kissed me and said I don't know what I was doing."

Holly's eyes widened. "Do you know what you are doing?"

"Well, no, but... Why would he say that?"

Why would you do such a thing? "I do not know, but why would you be kissing Bobby?"

"Because I like him." Tiffany spun around and faced Holly. "Isn't that what people do when they like one another?"

"Well, yes, but not until they are properly courting."

"If I wait for courting I will never kiss a boy. Have you?"

"Well, no, not yet."

"See. You are nearly twenty-one and never been kissed. That is just wrong." Tiffany crossed her arms.

"Tiff, why don't you tell me why you felt the need to be kissed by a boy that you do not love?"

"What do you mean?"

"Well, what drove you to want a kiss from Bobby? And if it did not matter who kissed you, why did you want to be kissed?"

"Bobby is all right. He was the best looking of the bunch."

"So you were with a group of others and kissed him. Was this a kind of a dare situation?"

"Sort of…not really. I don't see what all the fuss is about that I was kissing Bobby."

"The fuss is the reaction you felt after being kissed by a boy who then rejected your kisses. The reason I haven't kissed anyone yet—" her mind flashed back to the barn and the desire to kiss Bryce "—is that I feel my kisses are special. They are gifts to my husband, and only to him."

"Don't you want to practice first?"

Holly chuckled. "I think I would like to practice with my husband. We can learn together."

"Well, if your husband is Bryce, you won't be his first."

"What?"

"I heard Bryce telling his friend not to tell you about all the girls he dated in college. He told his friend he didn't kiss and tell."

"Oh. Well, I don't know if I will be marrying Bryce, or anyone for that matter, at this point in time."

"That is my point. I don't want to be an old maid like you. I want my own life, my own house, my own husband

and children. I am happy you are here taking care of all of us, but that isn't the kind of life I want for myself."

"And perhaps the good Lord will give you the desires of your heart. But how do you think your husband will feel to find out he isn't the first one to kiss you?"

"What do you mean?"

"Kisses are gifts of love, as are other intimate expressions of love to your spouse. I choose to save my gifts for my husband. I believe that is how God planned it for a husband and wife. The question is, do you see yourself as a precious gift for your spouse? Only you can give yourself to another. You choose what kind of gift you want to give to your spouse—one that's been used or one that is special and clean."

"You are talking about more than kisses, aren't you?"

"I am. And I know you learned from the same woman I did about your special gift for your husband."

Tiffany sighed. "Momma would not be pleased."

"No, she wouldn't. And I am not your mother, Tiff, so you need to tell Father what happened, and why. You need to decide if you are going to honor your spouse with an unused gift. I cannot do that for you. Only you can." Holly gave her sister a hug. "Wash your face and come on down for dinner in fifteen minutes. Father is in his den."

Holly prayed Father would understand the turmoil going on in Tiffany and not wring her neck. *She should know better. She does know better. She's just suffering from having her world knocked out from under her, like me,* Holly reflected.

Back in the kitchen she found Calvin standing on a soapbox washing his hands in the kitchen sink. "Did you string him up?"

"Yes 'em. I'll skin 'im tomorrow mornin' before school."

"I'll have a pot of rabbit stew for dinner tomorrow night."

"Thank you, Holly."

"You what?" Father's voiced boomed from his den.

"Uh-oh, who's in trouble now?" Calvin asked, wiping his hands on a towel. "I'm glad it isn't me this time."

Holly chuckled. "It could have been if Father had come in to see that rabbit on the counter."

"You won't tell him, will ya?"

"Not this time. But don't let it happen again."

"Yes 'em. I promise." Calvin ran off toward the back staircase, sneaking to his room away from his father's den.

"Holly Elizabeth, come in here," Father called out.

How is this going to be my fault?

Bryce headed his horse at an easy pace to Evergreen Cemetery to place a bouquet of flowers on Allison Graham's tombstone. Today marked the two-month anniversary of her passing. How his life had changed since then. She'd been his second mother. He loved her and missed her terribly, but his loss compared not a wit to the loss Holly and her family felt, of that he was certain. It had turned Holly's life—and his—topsy-turvy.

As he rounded the bend, his gaze settled on the rather shocking figure of Whit Butterfield kneeling in front of Mrs. Graham's freshly carved headstone. Bryce's grip tightened around the bouquet. Whit turned and acknowledged his approach.

"Excuse me, Bryce," Whit mumbled.

Bryce chose to stay in the saddle and look down at the man. "Why would you come here today?" he growled. "What if one of the Graham family came here? What would you have said to them? You don't have much sense in that head of yours, do you?"

"You have no right, Jarvis." The vein in the center of Whit's forehead bulged. "I have as much right to pay my respects as anyone. No matter what you or the rest of the world thinks about me. It's not your place to judge."

"But I have, and I find you lacking."

"And you don't think I do? Go ahead, have your say with Allison Graham. Pay your respects. But know this, you are no better than I." Whit placed his hat back on top of his head and stomped off.

Bryce knelt beside Allison's grave. "Forgive me, Allison." He sighed. "Forgive me, Lord."

"He's right, you know!" Bryce turned around to see who had spoken. "You are no better." A chill ran up his spine. No one was anywhere around. His conscience…his spirit…withered beneath the weight of God's voice. He was judgmental. And unforgiving. He was no better than Whit. He'd sinned on more than one occasion. The man was clearly seeking forgiveness for a senseless accident, and what did Bryce do? Judge his intentions.

Images of Holly flooded in his mind. He'd ruined all chances for them to get together. He'd been zealous in his desire to surprise her with the gift of a house. Yet with Allison gone, he'd been insensitive to her needs. His failing her when she'd asked for help hurt most of all. "Forgive me, Father. Forgive me, Allison."

He cried over the pain he'd caused others. He cried for the losses of Allison and Holly. He'd seek out Whit and apologize. He'd compose a letter and apologize to Holly. He cried for no particular reason at all. He stayed on his knees long enough that moisture from the ground now saturated his pant legs. Exhausted from the outburst of emotion he stood and placed the flowers. That is when he saw the stone that Holly had seen on the day of her mother's funeral. "Here lies Emmett Landers. Born 1840 Died 1862 during the war. Beloved Husband and Father."

"Why did Allison Graham leave the stone there once she knew he was still alive?" he muttered. He mounted his horse and headed back toward home. He continued to pray for guidance and understanding. Normally he was a patient man, even-tempered and not given to impulses, except around Holly. The first time he'd gotten into trouble because of her he was eleven and they had gathered a nest of baby field mice and brought them into the house. Mother had screamed. Holly had laughed and Bryce had pretended he was the great hunter tracking down every last one of them. Mother had not been amused. He'd taken full responsibility and Holly had never paid for that crime, at least not as far as he knew. There were many times when all of them ended up mucking stalls and doing some other smelly task in penance.

He, Catherine and Holly dubbed themselves the Three Musketeers until Chad turned eight and wanted to join in the fun. Then they were four. Most of their games were harmless. They playacted many of the stories in the woods they read about. Holly was Maid Marion to his Robin Hood. He never could convince her to play Juliet to his Romeo. And acting it out with his sister didn't hold quite the same appeal as it would have had Holly starred in the role.

Bryce's two-story home with Savannah-gray brick came into view. If Holly had seen the house, he knew she would have liked it. It fit her and her personality. The stairway up to the room above the carriage house held a small landing on top. He'd thought of playing Romeo and Juliet with Holly on those very stairs. He loved their childhood memories. "I have lost her, Father," he mumbled his final prayer. "Forgive me."

* * *

Holly breathed a sigh of relief leaving her father's den. He had not blamed her, after all. In fact, he'd been pleased with how she had handled Tiffany's situation. But it was clear more guidance for the children was needed. Their discussion led to the decision to secure a housekeeper. Holly would no longer have the sole responsibility of taking care of the family's day-to-day needs. He wanted her to focus on the issues that would arise from the children growing up. Tiffany was now restricted to the house from any activity besides school for the next week. Holly completely agreed with the punishment.

But the last comment he made upon her leaving the room still resonated in her memory. "You were right, child. We should have told you much sooner. I am sorry."

Her father had always been an even sort, a quality she liked in him, but apologies were few and far between. This one, she appreciated more than he knew. It calmed a piece of her that had been on edge since she'd returned from Tennessee. It made her see how she could thrive with two very different fathers in her life.

She served the family meal and everyone ate heartily. Calvin told of his adventures with his great rabbit hunt and the rest of the boys chimed in. Tiffany remained somber, only reacting when Holly gave her a smile every now and again.

As evening settled on the house, Holly realized she'd been avoiding Bryce. He had told her he would not approach her. If she wanted a relationship with him, she must take the first steps.

Did she want to? She wanted her dear friend back. She didn't feel ready for a suitor in her life, though. With her world so askew, she just couldn't feel much most of the time. When the feelings did come, the emotions were so strong and passionate she had a hard time controlling them.

In either case she feared Bryce. Which seemed utterly foolish.

She reached for her mother's Bible, the same one that had contained the letters. Her father Emmett had given it to her mother for Christmas the year before they married. She thumbed through the pages but nothing caught her interest. She knew she needed to talk with someone but the only person she wanted to talk to was Bryce. "God, what am I to do?"

She stopped at Proverbs 3:5-6. "Trust in the Lord with all thine heart; and lean not unto thine own understanding. In all thy ways acknowledge him, and he shall direct thy paths." She knew the verse well. Her mother had often quoted it. While she knew she should follow the teaching, a part of her needed more time to heal from the loss. Another part was afraid she would never feel any emotion again. She seemed numb. And yet she'd witnessed from a distance others who had lost someone and gone on with their lives. Were their lives buried in gray, too? Food lost its taste? Flowers their fragrance?

Her mind went to Bryce. Would it be so bad to be married to him? *He is handsome. He cares for me. We talk well with one another. He'd be a good provider.* How many men were able to buy a house at twenty-three years old? Not many, she supposed.

Holly was more confused and conflicted than ever. The verse in Proverbs did little to quiet her churning mind. Finally she prepared an early breakfast for the family, then rode into town before the sun rose.

A two-story house with a carriage house on the property and near Forsythe Park totaled the little she knew of Bryce's home.

As the sun rose in the east she saw the folly in her quest. If she had simply waited a bit longer she could have asked Catherine or even his family for his address. Instead she'd run on impulse. She directed the horse to stop the gig at the southeast corner of Forsythe Park. "Father God, I seem more impulsive these days. And you seem more distant. I need someone to talk to. In truth, I need Bryce."

She mumbled her prayer and sat. Birdsong filled the morning air. The creak of the leather harness as the horse came to a complete stop caused her to pause and take in the still surroundings. Some folks were heading to work. Servants into the larger homes that lined the park entered through the rear or side entrances. Men dressed in black suits with white starched shirts exited through the front doors and headed north toward the wharfs, exchange and banks to begin their day. But no sign of Bryce. More than likely he'd be heading from town to his family home in a short while. Perhaps she could catch him there.

Holly eased the horse backward and then pivoted the horse and gig to turn to the right and down a side street.

"Holly Graham, is that you?" a woman's voice shrieked from off to her left.

She pulled back the reins and guided the horse to a stop.

"Well, I'll be. Where you comin' from at this hour? It's good to see you."

"Jessie?" She and Jessie had attended school together. Jessie had graduated a year before Holly.

"Sure 'nough. Hey, I heard about your mother, I'm so sorry. How are you? And what has you in town so early in the morning?"

"Couldn't sleep, and thank you."

"Ain't never lost no one close to me but my ma did and she had a difficult time sleeping. So, I suppose you is normal."

Holly smiled. Jessie never had learned to use grammar and proper speech, even after years in fine schools. She was, however, an upstanding and honest person. "Thank you. I don't feel normal."

"I suspect you won't for a long time. How's the rest of the family?"

"We're each dealing with it in our own way. Father is trying to hold everything together, but he is relying on me to help raise the kids."

"Reckon that would be your job."

"Is this your home?"

"Goodness, no. Me and my husband have a small place south of here. I've been told there is a house for sale and I thought I'd check it out."

Holly's heart quickened. "Which house? Who's the owner?"

"Bryce Jarvis. His sister Catherine and I were in the same grade. You knew her, right?"

"Yes. Where's the house?" She didn't want to give the appearance of being overly interested in Bryce.

"Just down here a bit. Bryce said if I came early he'd show me the place. My husband, Jeff Turner, well, he had to go to work and said I should look it over before he does. If it don't fit my needs, then well, why would he need to waste his time?"

"Do you mind if I join you?"

"Be a pleasure, another set of eyes, you know what I mean. Mr. Bryce, he said he bought the place in disrepair, but Catherine said he fixed it up real nice. Catherine gave me the impression that he purchased the place for himself and a future wife but apparently their relationship didn't work out. Jeff's hoping it is within our price range. He's not one to take advantage of a man down on his luck but he's not against a bargain, either."

Holly's hands started to shake. She wanted to see Bryce but coming with a woman who was inquiring to buy the house he'd purchased for them... She didn't want to hurt him further. "You know, I probably should get home and make certain my siblings head off to school."

"Ah, well, know that you've been in my prayers."

"Thank you, Jessie. It means a lot."

"You're more than welcome. Give my regards to your family."

"I will." Holly jiggled the reins. The horse eased forward.

Jessie walked toward her goal.

A desire to see Bryce and the house grew. She closed her eyes and contemplated stopping again.

"Holly, are you all right?" Jessie's steps quickened.

Holly pulled back on the reins. "Jessie, would you give Mr. Jarvis a message for me?"

"Sure."

She licked her lips. Asking Jessie meant letting others know. "Tell him Miss Landers would like to see him."

"Be happy to."

Holly gave a weak smile and a wave. "Thank you. Have a blessed day."

Jessie beamed. "I surely am hoping to."

Holly headed south; away from the man she would have loved to spend the day with. She was headed home, but the place no longer felt the same. All the comfort of the past was lost with her mother. Comfort and calm were replaced with anxiety and lack of sleep. Did death have to be so exhausting?

Chapter 9

Bryce held the door open for Jessie Turner. He hesitated at the thought of potential buyers entering his home. But Catherine had mentioned the house to a friend, and Bryce realized the house had been ready to show for weeks. He'd been holding on to a hope that maybe Holly would change her mind. She'd been home for several weeks and he had not heard one word from her. Whatever hope he'd had diminished a little each day.

"Thank you for coming so early." Bryce closed the door behind them.

"Pleased to do it. Before I forget, I just saw Holly Graham and she asked me to pass on a message to ya that a Miss Landers would like to see you."

His pulse quickened. "Thank you. Where did you see Miss Graham?"

"On Park Avenue. She's havin' a rough time with the loss of her mother. My, my, the pain she must be sufferin' from. She's such a sweet girl, takin' care of her family. Of course, you know all that. I forget you're neighbors."

"Yes, I know the Graham family. So, shall I show you the house?"

He wanted to jump on his horse and run off after Holly and not show his house. Not sleeping, early morning rides alone in the city didn't bode well for Holly. These were not healthy choices for a young woman to make.

After a brief tour of the house Jessie asked, "I know this might sound strange, Mr. Jarvis, but would it be all right if I's can stay around for a bit longer, see if I can get a feel for the place? Jeff and I want to start a family and, well, I needs to know if we will feel comfortable here."

"Normally I would say no. However, since you're such a good friend of my sister's, I'd be happy to let you wander around a bit. Sit a spell in the garden, there's so much more that could be done to that area. I will not be able to stay, I'm sorry to say. There is some business I must attend to right away."

A smile lit up Jessica's rosy cheeks. "I understand. Thank you."

Bryce felt certain he'd made a sale and the heavy yoke around his neck might soon be lifted. Holly's thinly veiled message, on the other hand, reignited a quivering hope that possibly, just possibly, she still wanted to be a part of his life. He raced to the carriage house and led his horse out, having saddled him earlier for a ride. Spurring the animal into a gallop, he left the house behind in a cloud of dust.

As he approached the turn-off to his family's plantation he could see Holly riding ahead in the gig. He brought the horse to a halt. Overzealousness had already pushed her away once. Reluctantly he turned the horse toward the plantation, deciding to write a note instead. Perhaps that would help him gain some control over his emotions.

The entire weight of Holly's anguish began to settle on his heart. How had he not seen this before? In the midst of her grief and confusion he had thrust his plans, his desires and his dreams for their future upon her. Holly needed the security of his friendship, and he had left her feeling manipulated, controlled and alone.

Once at the house he went straight to the den, penned a brief message, sealed it with wax and pressed his ring into the seal. He would give it to one of the hands to deliver to the Graham estate.

His mother's bright voice fell like sunshine on his heavy mood. "Good morning, son. You're in early."

Bryce looked up from his desk to see his mother in the doorway. "I showed Mrs. Turner the house, and she asked to spend some time alone to get a feel for the place."

His mother cocked her right eyebrow. "That's unusual."

Bryce shrugged and pushed himself up from his desk. "Anyone heading to the Grahams' today?"

"I'll be going. It seems John will be taking appointments for a housekeeper today."

"Oh? Isn't that Holly's job?"

"It will give Holly a break so she can help with the children."

Bryce wagged his head from side to side. "Don't you think the parenting should belong solely on Mr. Graham's shoulders?"

"Normally I'd agree, but apparently Tiffany has…" Her words trailed off.

He saw the concern and embarrassment in his mother's face. "Has she been harmed?" he asked, coming to his feet. He'd take care of anyone who took advantage of one of the Graham children.

His mother raised her hand. "She's fine, more or less. Oh phooey, you might as well know. Tiffany kissed a boy and John is all upset about it. Apparently she wanted to be kissed but the boy made fun of her afterward."

Bryce's thoughts raced back to the awkward, sometimes painful experiences with girls during his school years. "Was she looking for a relationship or simply a kiss?"

"Hard to say. John admits he was so beside himself he didn't hear everything she told him. Thankfully, she'd spoken with Holly first and got some good advice. Holly even sent Tiffany in to confess to her father."

"She is a remarkable woman."

His mother smiled. "Why did you ask?"

Bryce thought back on the myriad occasions he and Holly had had conversations over the years about male-female relationships—what was proper, what was not... "Ask? Ask what?"

"You asked if someone was going to the Grahams'."

"Oh, sorry. This news about Tiffany startled me. I have a note for Holly, if you wouldn't mind taking it over."

"I don't believe John will give you any further trouble, Bryce. I'm sure he's forgiven you by now."

How could he explain to his mother? "That isn't the problem. The message is best delivered this way."

"All right, if you say so. If you want my opinion, though, you need to see her and speak with her personally. You cannot keep blaming yourself for her reactions following the death of her mother."

"I know. But she sent word that she would like me to contact her, so I'm simply replying."

"By a note rather than in person?"

"It's appropriate, Mother."

"Fine. I'll step away and let you handle your own affairs. You've been doing that for quite some time now."

"You're not still upset that I moved out, are you?"

"No, dear. It was time. I just wish… Oh, I don't know what I wish. You purchased a house without our knowledge—not that you had to tell us, of course… But why the secret?"

"As I told you and Father before, it was a foolish desire to surprise Holly. I won't be making that mistake again."

"And why the active social life, all of a sudden?"

"Mother, please."

"Oh, all right. But you are making a mistake. You are not going to find the woman you are looking for when you already know who she is. Be patient, son. That is all I'm suggesting."

Bryce sighed. "Patience is the reason for this note."

"See, that wasn't that hard to admit, was it?"

Bryce chuckled. "Touché."

His mother came over and embraced him in a bear hug. "I love you, son."

"I know. And I love you, too."

She parted with a tap on his shoulder. "I shall deliver your note."

Bryce nodded. He had moved out on his own, at least in part, to create some distance from his parents' meddling in his life. He realized now that such a time would never come, not unless he moved away from Savannah. While that was not a real option, of course, it did offer the benefit of no longer confronting his lost love.

But what about the message from Mrs. Turner? Knowing now what he'd learned about Tiffany, perhaps that was all Holly wanted to talk with him about. Bryce sucked in a deep breath, bracing himself for the inevitable encounter that would amount to nothing more than offering brotherly advice. "Why didn't I tell her how I really felt about her back in college?" he muttered out loud.

"Tell who what?" Chad asked as he sauntered into the office.

"Holly, my dear!" Cynthia Jarvis called out as she entered the kitchen. "How are you?"

"Fine, thank you, and you?"

"Fine. Oh, before I forget." She pulled an envelope out from her skirt pocket. "Bryce asked me to give you this."

Holly reached out to receive the proffered note. "Thank you. How is he?"

"He's doing well." Cynthia grabbed an apron from its wall hook and tied it on. "Your father has asked me to help interview potential housekeepers. Will you be involved with the interviews, as well?"

"Father hasn't asked for my input." Holly traced the wax imprint made from Bryce's ring. "Will you excuse me for a moment?"

"Certainly." Cynthia Jarvis went to the stove. "Rabbit stew?"

"Yes, Calvin insisted again. He likes his hunting, but I'm tired of the rabbit stew and I know his brothers are, too."

"He probably finds comfort in the hunting. Something to put his mind on rather than thinking about missing his mother."

"Yes, I believe you are right but… It doesn't matter. We'll eat the stew."

Cynthia smiled and picked up where she'd left off the last time she was in the kitchen, drying herbs and preparing the household for winter. Holly didn't mind. It was one less thing she needed to concern herself with. A few short months ago her life seemed so carefree. Now… Holly fingered the letter and headed up to her room. She broke the seal and read.

> Dear Holly,
> Jessie Turner said she'd run into you and asked that I get in touch with you. As you are well aware, I have moved into the city. I reside on the corners of Broadway and East Park Ave. You can send your correspondence there. I am at your service in whatever capacity you need me to be.
> Affectionately,
> Bryce

Holly read the short missive one more time. What was she hoping to find? She had only asked that he get in touch with her, and he had. Did she expect him to declare his love for her? At least he stated he would be available. "What do you want from him?" she chided herself and began to pace in her room. She wanted more. She wanted him, his friendship, their long conversations about everything and nothing at all.

"Dear God, help me."

Holly collapsed into the reading chair and looked out the window. The river flowed eternally by, bright and peaceful. Her thoughts drifted away in its hypnotic current until the tree-studded banks turned into a canal in Venice, Italy. She could feel the misty breeze on her face as her gondola glided along, the gondolier at the stern with his long paddle, and Bryce reclined beside her. A sigh of longing passed over her parted lips with the realization that she loved him. She had always loved him, wanted him, even envied him. The mystical canal swirled back to the river she knew so well, and to the present. An overwhelming sense of determination swelled up within her. She had loved Bryce for as long as she could remember. She would do whatever it took to get him back in her life.

Holly stood, went to her dressing table and straightened her hair. She would meet Tiffany at school and take her shopping, then bring her home. After that she would follow her heart and try to establish a relationship with Bryce once again.

Holly left her room for the carriage house, prepared the Jenny Lind buggy and set off to take care of her responsibilities with Tiffany. She then proceeded on her mission to find Bryce at his home on the corner of Broadway and East Park Avenue. What she didn't expect to find was Jessie and Jeff Turner examining his house.

"Holly, twice in one day," Jessie called out.

"Hello again, Jessie. So, you liked the house?"

"Yes 'em. He did a mighty fine job restoring the old place. Most of the houses here are fairly new, but this one has been around for nearly eighty years. It has a larger piece of property and, well, you must know all about it."

"No, I haven't visited here before." Holly suddenly realized her missed opportunity. "Is Mr. Jarvis home?"

"No, I'm afraid not. I brought Jeff here right from work." Jessie tugged on her husband's sleeve and introduced him. "Jeff, this is Holly Graham. Holly, this here is my husband, Jeff Turner. He's not from around here. He's actually a Yank, but I don't hold it against him."

Jeff chuckled, and Holly smiled. "Pleasure to meet you, Mr. Turner." She extended her hand. He received it with refinement.

"Pleasure is all mine, Miss Graham."

"Actually, my name is Landers. I'm going by my given name these days."

"Landers? Given name? Do tell?" Jessie came closer to the buggy.

"Nothing much to tell. My mother was married before she met John Graham. We used Graham so as not to confuse teachers, the other children and so on."

"So your father died?" Jessie asked.

"Jessica," Jeff chided.

"Sorry, I didn't mean to…well, actually, I did. What happened, if you don't mind me knowing?"

"It isn't a secret." Holly briefly and matter-of-factly explained about her mother's first marriage.

"Well, goodness me! I never would have guessed such a thing."

And Holly never thought she'd be explaining all this. However, if she wasn't going to continue the secret, she knew she would be explaining the story again and again. No one needed to know that it had been a shock to her, as well.

"Oh, wait, you had me pass on a message to Bryce this morning from a Miss Landers. So that would be you?"

"Yes." Holly secured the reins and eased out of the buggy. Jeff Turner extended a hand to help balance her.

"Do ya know if Mr. Jarvis will be returning soon?" Jessie asked. "I was hoping to show Jeff the house with Bryce here."

"I honestly don't know." Holly walked around to the rear of the buggy and lifted the basket of prepared food she had brought for her and Bryce.

Jeff took his wife's hand. "It appears Mr. Jarvis will be having company this evening. We can return again."

The sound of a galloping horse caught everyone's attention. Holly smiled at the sight of Bryce. He stiffened noticeably in his saddle when he recognized her. "Hello," he called out. His glance shifted to the basket and back to her and then to Jessie and Jeff. "Is there an evening affair at the park tonight?"

"No." Jessie smiled. "Jeff and I were wondering if we could see the house. And Holly...well, she has some other kind of plans I'd say."

Holly felt the heat rise on her cheeks.

"The wife and I will take our leave, Mr. Jarvis. She is very excited about your home. Shall we plan another time for a closer inspection?"

"That would be fine, Mr. Turner." Bryce and Jeff shook hands and the couple headed toward the park.

"Holly?"

"I'm sorry, Bryce. I wanted to speak with you and, well, they were here and, well...oh goodness, I'm beside myself here. I told Jessie who I was. I need you, Bryce. I've missed you so much."

He stepped forward and put his arm around her. "Shh, it's all right. I've missed you, too. Come on, let me put my horse away and then you can show me what's in your basket."

Relief washed over Holly. He wasn't so angry with her that he didn't want to spend some time with her. "I hope you're hungry. I brought a little of everything."

"I'm famished. Whatever you brought will be fine."

"We did have a full pot of rabbit stew but I've had my fill of that this past month. Calvin has become quite the hunter."

Bryce chuckled. "I do miss that little man."

They entered the barn and Bryce made quick work of removing the saddle and setting up fresh oats. He then proceeded to give his horse a good brush-down.

"It appears that Jessie loves the house," Holly remarked, instantly regretting it. A look of sadness spread across his face. "I am sorry. I meant it as a compliment. She went on and on about the place and…"

He held up his hand. "It's all right, Holly. I understand your lack of interest in the house."

"No, Bryce, it isn't that at all." She paused, considering her words carefully. "We need to talk, but I think what we need to say to one another will hurt. Let's agree not to walk away from each other in anger."

Bryce laughed. "That will be harder for you than me. You do realize what you are suggesting?"

"I do, and you're right. I will have the harder time. On the other hand, even anger will feel a lot better than what I've been feeling for the past month."

His hand paused with the brush on the horse's hindquarters. "What have you been feeling?"

"Nothing. I am going through life with no emotions at all. I'm doing everything that is required of me and yet I feel no joy, no pain, no anything. I am numb."

"Sorry to hear that. Have you talked with the pastor or perhaps someone else who's lost a family member?"

"No. Today is the first day I've actually left the house since my return from Tennessee."

"Jessie told me about meeting you on the street this morning. You must have gotten down here before the sun rose."

"I did. I was hoping to find you. But I didn't know where to find your house, and when I met Jessie I thought I could simply follow her. Then she mentioned how you had purchased it for a wife, but that didn't work out and, well…the guilt got the best of me."

He placed the horse brush back on the shelf and stepped out of the stall. "Holly, please don't feel badly about the house. I know now I should have waited to tell you. I wanted to help, and instead I made your burden worse. For that I am profoundly sorry. Can you forgive me?"

"Forgive you? Goodness, it is I that needs to ask for your forgiveness. I ran off on you to Tennessee. Since coming home I haven't had the energy— No, that's not completely true. I haven't even had the desire to see you. No, that's not exactly true, either. I have the desire but I don't trust myself. My emotions are up and down, excited then nothing at all. Mostly they are nothing. I hate feeling nothing. Trust me, angry is a whole lot better than nothing."

"Come, let us go into the house," Bryce said with a sweep of his hand toward the side door. "I will give you a brief tour, then we can sit down and enjoy whatever you brought for supper."

"I'd like that."

He offered his hand and she took it. She'd held Bryce's hands on many occasions over the years. Tonight felt different. "Come, your honor is safe with me."

She blushed. "I know."

The tour ended in the dining room, where he pulled a chair from the table for her.

"Thank you, Bryce," she said, taking her seat. "The house is marvelous. You've done a great job. You are right, I would have loved it."

He took the chair opposite hers. "Thank you. Now…" He rubbed his hands together in eager anticipation. "What did you bring in that basket?"

Chapter 10

"Holly, we have a problem," Bryce said over his shoulder from the front door. He couldn't believe his eyes. A dense fog quilted the ground beneath a moonless night. Darkness, thicker than he'd ever seen it before, swallowed the tree-lined road. "You cannot drive home in this. It isn't safe."

Fear filled her eyes. "I have already pushed Father's patience by insisting I am quite capable of visiting you for an evening without ruining my reputation. What are we going to do?"

"You are going to spend the night here and I will make my way to my parents' house. I am safer on a horse. I will put your buggy and horse in the carriage house for the night."

"What if I rode the horse home and you escorted me?"

"That would be better than you going alone. But still, I would feel much better if you spent the night here while I go to my parents'."

"Yes, but whoever comes looking for me in the morning will find me here alone. I do not think that would be wise."

"Perhaps you are right. I will get the horses ready. Can you ride in that dress?"

"Yes, if you lend me scissors or a knife and give me some privacy."

Bryce didn't want to even imagine what Holly had in mind. He knew she could ride like a man. She'd done it many times when they were children. But in a dress? He shook his head. "I shall ready the horses. You do whatever you have to do."

He left as if fire nipped at his heels. They had enjoyed such a good evening together. Their conversation revolved somewhat around their relationship, and the death of her mother, but mostly around Holly's fear of not being able to feel again. "Father," Bryce had prayed, holding her hands, "please, give her strength and guidance."

Holly entered the carriage house and saw that he had the first horse saddled. "All set," she proclaimed, indicating her altered dress. "It isn't pretty, but it will work."

Bryce took her word for it without looking. "I will ride bareback," he said. He had forgotten about not having another saddle when agreeing to serve as her escort. "Give me a minute. I will be right back." He re-entered the house and pulled out his hunting rifle and a Colt 45 pistol. He stuffed his sheathed hunting knife inside his boot.

Outside, he met the black shadow that was Holly astride her horse. "Shall we?"

"You are right, Bryce, it is really dark out here."

"Never seen it this dark. Come on, let's go." Bryce grabbed hold of the horse's withers and swung himself up. It felt odd not to have a saddle under him. But he'd ridden bareback enough over the years that gripping with his thighs didn't take much effort.

They made their way down the city streets without much problem as streetlamps and house lamps helped light the way. Once outside the city limits, utter darkness enveloped them once again.

"Bryce?"

"Hmm?" he answered, keeping himself alert to the road and their surroundings.

"I don't mind telling you I'm afraid."

Bryce smiled. "That's good. Fear is an emotion. Not a pleasant one, but an emotion."

Holly laughed. "Thanks, I feel much better now."

"Don't even give it another consideration. I don't need constant praise."

"Right, and there's a full moon out tonight," she teased.

"There is? I cannot find it. Can you?"

"The air doesn't feel right."

"No, feels like a storm, or worse. A cyclone might be getting ready to blow through. You know what to do if we have a funnel cloud or cyclone come down, right?"

"Lie in a ditch."

"Right." They continued on in silence.

"Bryce?"

"Yeah?"

Before she could speak, someone jumped out in front of them and cocked his gun. "Hang on there, this here is a holdup."

"You've got to be kidding," Holly squealed. "Of all the stupid things to do on a night like this. How do you know we don't have a group of men following us right now?"

"What?" The would-be robber stepped toward Holly.

Bryce came off his horse with a kick toward the man's head. He went down. Bryce stood over the man and kicked his gun away. "Holly, get me some rope so I can tie him up."

"Where will I find some?"

Bryce thought for a moment. "Sorry, I did not pack the saddlebags."

"He's not going to get up for a little while. Why don't we just head on home?"

"No, I don't trust him. He might have friends. I will tie him up with my shirt and pick him up in the morning." He removed his shirt and made strips of cloth to bind the man's hands and feet. *What if he has partners nearby?* Bryce wondered to himself. "Holly, do you have a petticoat on under your dress?"

"Yes. I have a slip that goes down to the hem of my dress."

"Even better. Let me have a few inches off the bottom." Holly got down from the horse and lifted her skirt slightly. Bryce cut off a three-inch strip. "Thank you. Now get back in the saddle. I don't want you without an escape if he has buddies out here."

Holly silently obeyed.

"Hey, Tom, where are ya?" someone whispered in the dark.

Bryce sprang to Holly's side and jumped up behind her on the horse, slapping him to a full gallop. He grabbed her waist with both hands, but the saddle's hard cantle pounded against him, forcing him backward on the horse's rump.

"Hang on, Bryce!" Holly whipped the reins against the beast's heaving flanks and got a bit more speed out of him.

The loud crack of gunfire pierced the thick night air. Hot lead slammed into his back. He moaned but held on. It shouldn't take more than a few more minutes at this speed to be at his parents' plantation. "My house," he groaned.

"If I can find the road." A flash of lightning illuminated their path. Bryce turned to see if they were still being pursued.

"I saw your lane, Bryce. We're almost there. Hold on."

"I am." The winds began to pick up. Bryce could feel the blood oozing from the wound. "Holly, I love you."

"I love you, too, Bryce. Were you hit?"

"Yes."

"Hang on. I can see a light from your house." She used it as a guide and within minutes she was at the front door. Bryce released his grip and slid to the ground with a heavy thud. "Bryce!" she screamed, scurrying to his side. "Bryce, stay with me."

Lights brightened in the house. Holly grabbed hold of him and put his arm around her shoulders. "Help, Bryce is hurt," she yelled. The front door flew open. Chad barreled down the stairs, with Ryan right behind him. "What happened?"

"Bandits on the road. He's been shot."

"I will fetch the doctor." Ryan jumped up on the horse and raced back to the city.

Lloyd and Cynthia came out as their son galloped off.

"Bryce has been shot. Looks bad," Chad told his parents.

"Get him inside," Lloyd ordered. "Cynthia, boil a couple of pots of water. Michael, fetch Bryce's animal husbandry tools. Chad, you and Holly lay him on the dining room table. Gather as many lamps as you can. We'll need a few mirrors, as well," Lloyd ordered.

Once they had Bryce on the table, Holly saw the ugly wound. Her pulse drummed in her ears. The food in her stomach spoiled. "Holly, get some towels. Chad—the lights."

"Yes, sir."

"Lloyd Jarvis," Cynthia exclaimed. "You are a lawyer, for heaven's sake! What do you know about doctoring?"

"Seen enough wounds during the war. First thing is to clean it out. Do you have any silk thread, Cynthia?"

"Yes."

"Good. Fetch that, and get your sharpest needles and a pair of pliers."

"Dear God in heaven, you're going to operate?" Cynthia went deathly pale and crumpled to the floor.

"Holly, help Cynthia."

"Yes, sir." Holly placed the towels on one of the chairs beside the table.

"Chad, rearrange the hutch so that we can set up mirrors to hang off the top at an angle. Make the light reflect down at your brother. Use wire, string…whatever it takes." Lloyd grabbed a towel and pressed it on Bryce's back.

Bryce screamed, then passed out again. "Good, son. Hang in there, boy. You are going to be fine. It's a clean wound."

Holly marveled at the strength and fortitude Mr. Jarvis displayed for his family. The kettle in the kitchen whistled, signaling that the water had boiled. Michael came running in with Bryce's tools.

"Take that knife and those pliers and put them in the boiling water, Michael."

"Yes, sir."

"Leave them in there until the water starts to boil again. Then we need to time it for ten minutes."

"Yes, sir."

Lloyd lifted the blood-soaked towel and tossed it aside. "Pour some hot water on this towel. Then grab a pitcher of cold water to cleanse this wound, Holly."

"Yes, sir." Holly trembled but went straight to work. It was easy to follow orders from someone who knew what they were doing. "You could have been a surgeon, Mr. Jarvis."

"Not likely," he replied. He glanced back at his wife who still remained passed out. "Cynthia, wake up. I need you. Bryce needs you, honey. Come on, honey. Wake up, please."

Cynthia began to stir as Holly came up beside Mr. Jarvis with a pitcher of water. "Pour it on the wound until I say stop."

Holly nodded and applied the cool liquid on the open wound. Blood and grit flowed down his sides onto the table and floor below. "Perfect. Stop pouring for a moment." Lloyd applied more pressure with a clean towel.

"Cynthia, are you able to get me that thread and needle now?" His tender tone touched Holly.

"Water is boiling again, Dad," Michael called from the kitchen.

"Great, check the clock and watch for ten minutes."

"Yes, sir."

"You are doing a great job on the lights, Chad."

"I'll have the mirrors tied up in a couple minutes."

"Excellent work, son." Lloyd removed the towel. It wasn't as saturated as the previous one. "Good, the bleeding is slowing down."

Bryce moaned.

"Holly, put the pitcher of water down. In my den, in the bottom drawer on the right side, is a bottle of whiskey. Would you fetch it, please?"

"Yes, sir."

Father kept the whiskey in the same place in his den. Every household had a bottle for medicinal purposes. It seemed odd to rummage in another man's desk, but then again, for Bryce, she'd do anything. Finding the clear-glass bottle, she ran back to the dining area. Cynthia was coming down the stairs, still a little pale but able to hold her own.

"Take a sip, Cynthia. I'm going to need you to help me."

Cynthia opened the bottle, sipped, then coughed violently. "How horrifying!"

Lloyd chuckled. "That's my girl. Come on. I am going to need you to help Bryce.

"Chad, when you're done with those mirrors, I am going to need you to help remove your brother's trousers. Ladies, turn your backs then."

"How's that?" Chad asked.

"Excellent, son. Come, let's get him set up for surgery. Take off his boots, then his pants. Then we will cover him with a sheet. Michael, run upstairs and get a sheet for your brother."

"Yes, sir."

The men worked quickly and Bryce was clean and covered again in no time. "How much longer on those instruments, Michael?"

"I'll check." Michael ran back to the kitchen.

Lloyd lifted the towel. "The bleeding is almost stopped. We can wait for the doctor. I would hate to go in there and cause the bleeding to start up again. After all, I am not a surgeon."

"Maybe not, but you can help work on me anytime," Chad said to encourage his father.

"Me, too," Michael chimed in. "How do I get the tools out of the water, Dad?"

"Pour boiling water on one of Mom's cooking sheets then drain it in the sink. Use your mother's wooden tongs and pick out the tools one at a time and place them on the clean baking sheets."

"Yes, sir."

"Holly, hold this towel firmly on the wound. Chad, help me lift the table under the chandelier."

The front door flung open. "Doc says he'll be here as soon as possible. He says to hold a clean towel on the wound…" Ryan's words trailed off. "Apparently ya'll are already doing that."

Holly smiled.

"Ryan, clean the sweat off then hold the towel on Bryce's wound. Holly, I want you to feed the whiskey to Bryce. Drip it on his tongue. Try to get him to swallow some before the doctor gets here."

"Yes, sir." Instead, Cynthia Jarvis stood at the head of the table. She opened her hand and without saying a word asked for the whiskey. Holly handed it to her and sat after Ryan took her place. In the heat of the emergency Holly felt a strange surge of energy and clarity of thought. As the pace slowed, however, she felt the room begin to swirl. She closed her eyes then opened and focused straight ahead. The room no longer swayed.

Bryce woke to throbbing pain in his back. He reached behind to find a bandage and saw the doctor standing over him.

"You have quite a father there, son," the doctor said. "If I didn't know him to be so good at law, I'd suggest he missed his calling. You're going to have a fever fighting off the infection, but you'll be fine. Your father cleansed the wound well and I had excellent light for surgery."

What was he talking about? The last thing he remembered was tying up a bandit… He tried to jump up. "Holly! Where's Holly? Was she hurt?" The strong arms of the doctor held him down.

"She's fine. The only one injured was you." The doctor closed his valise. "I will give your parents instructions for your care. You won't remember them even if I did tell you."

Bryce chuckled then stopped. Pain shot through his back.

"Well, you gave us quite a scare tonight," Chad said

as he came into the room and sat beside the bed. "What happened?"

"Bandits."

"Holly told us that much. Ryan said he saw your horse on the side of the road but there was no one tied up there."

"He had a partner. At least one, possibly two, I think. I honestly don't know. What did Holly say?"

"Not too much, apart from you being this incredible hero straight out of a novel. As if you were one of the Knights of the Round Table or Robin Hood. And truthfully, if you did what she said you did, you did sound rather remarkable. Even if you are my brother."

Breathless, Chad related the tale of how the family had come together to tend to Bryce's wound. Then he turned to the matter of the bandits. "Ryan and I will go to the sheriff's in the morning and report the crime. He'll probably want to come talk with you after that."

Bryce nodded.

"What were you doing out with Holly on such a dark night?'

"I was escorting her home."

"But…"

Bryce shot Chad a glare that warned him not to ask further.

"All right, I won't ask. She's asleep in Catherine's old room. Her dress was all torn. Did that happen from the bandits?"

"No, she did that herself in order to ride home rather than drive her buggy."

"Ah." Chad tapped him on the shoulder. "I'll let you get some more sleep. The sun will be coming up soon. I need to check to see if the storm did any damage."

Bryce nodded once again as his father walked into the room.

"How you doing, son?"

"Better. Apparently thanks to you, Dad. To hear Chad tell, it you were…incredible. Thank you."

"You would have done the same. I am going to retire for what is left of the evening. I wanted to stop in and check on you first. Your mother is anxious to see you, as well."

"Send her in."

His father nodded and exited the room. His mother's eyes were red and swollen as she entered and approached the bed, but the smile on her face encouraged him. "I will be all right, Mom."

"I know you will and I have been thanking the good Lord all night. Holly said it was all her fault for encouraging you to escort her home. Personally, I don't believe it."

"It wasn't her fault. If she hadn't been there with me there's no telling if I would be alive right now."

His mother nodded in agreement. "I'll reassure her in the morning. At first light, Michael is going to ride over to the Grahams' and let them know what happened. I hope John has gotten some sleep. More than likely he's been up all night worried."

Bryce agreed. Pain gripped him and he let out a moan. "Sorry."

"The doctor said you will have some pain for a while. What really needs watching, however, is the fever as your body fights off infection."

"I understand. I will try to be a good patient."

His mother bent and kissed his forehead. "Try and get some sleep, son. That will help you recover."

"Yes, ma'am." Bryce closed his eyes and sleep overtook him until sunlight poured through his bedroom windows. He woke with a start from dark dreams, drenched in sweat beneath the heavy covers in the heat of the new day, and stripped the blankets off.

Holly sprang from a rocking chair in the corner of the room. "Bryce, stop! Bryce, honey, stop!"

Strangely enough, her excited voice calmed him.

"What is happening?"

"You're running a fever. You have been asleep for a day." She dipped a cloth in a basin of fresh water, wrung it out and placed it on his forehead. She repeated the process on his throat, shoulders and chest. "You are feverish from the infection."

"Holly, I love you."

"I love you, too."

He lifted his arms and wrapped them around her neck and pulled her down. "Bryce, stop," she whispered in alarm. "Not now."

He opened his eyes and realized he wasn't dreaming. "Sorry. I…I…"

"Shh. You are forgiven." She glanced over her shoulder and, seeing they were still alone, leaned close to his face and whispered, "I'll be interested in kissing you later when you are feeling better."

"Promise?"

Holly's smile in return touched his heart.

"I promise, Bryce. Remember the night in the barn when I wanted to kiss you?"

He nodded.

"You said you would wait until I knew for certain what kind of love I have for you. I know now. So now I am asking you to wait until you are fully recovered. You said you wanted it to be special, and I do, too."

He released her. "Absolutely. Until then I shall continue to dream."

Holly giggled. "And so will I."

Bryce groaned. "You are sure you want to wait? I wouldn't mind kissing you right now."

"But I would!" John Graham's harsh voice boomed throughout the room.

Chapter 11

Holly straightened and turned to see her father standing in Bryce's doorway. "You should have knocked."

"You are in no position…"

She held up a hand to stop him from going further. "Not now. Bryce needs his rest. Are you here to apply the cool compresses? If so, I could use a break."

Frustration oozed out of every pore from her father's face. She was pushing him away and he knew it. Then there was the matter of trying to regain control of her own life.

"I'll be happy to apply the compresses."

"I'll be back after I take care of a few things." She whispered in his ear, "Father, I still love you."

Her father nodded, removed his jacket and sat next to the bed.

"Sorry, sir."

"Bryce, I'm here to apologize for my behavior since

Holly left for Tennessee. I can see now she's determined to make her own choices, and Tennessee was her choice."

Bryce blinked in acknowledgment.

"Holly told me all about the other night. I am sorry my daughter's willful behavior caused this."

"No, sir. If Holly hadn't been there I might not be alive today."

John paused. "I hadn't thought about it that way. She explained the options the two of you faced. And while I wouldn't have been pleased with her spending the night in your house, even with you not there, it seemed the logical plan to escort her home. In the future, if something like that were to happen again, convince her to stay at your place."

"Yes, sir. Her honor is safe with me."

"Does that include kissing?"

Bryce's face flamed. "Sorry, sir."

"Promise me you'll love and respect her as every woman has the right to be cherished."

"Yes, sir."

"Good. You have my blessings."

"Thank you, sir."

"Now let me see. I'm supposed to refresh this cloth and wring it out before putting it on you, correct?"

"Yes, sir."

Holly, leaning against the wall in the hallway just outside the door, smiled. It may not have been as formal as Bryce might have liked, but she knew that Father had just given Bryce permission to court her. She eased away and headed down the hall. She did have some necessary chores to attend to.

"How's Bryce?" Catherine asked as they approached one another on the stairs. "He's awake. My father is with him now."

"I will relieve him. Why don't you take a break, eat something, take a nap? Mom said you have been at his side all day."

"I'm fine. But I am going to take a break. Thank you."

John Graham walked into the parlor and gave a light knock on the doorjamb. "Holly, may I have a word with you?"

"Yes, Father, give me a moment." Holly put down the sandwich she was eating and covered it with a cloth. "What do you need?"

He took a seat opposite her on the sofa. "Time with my daughter."

"Forgive me, Father, but Bryce needs me."

"I know, and I am glad that the two of you are finding your way. I do miss our personal conversations, however. They were few, I admit that, but…"

"Ever since I left and returned from Tennessee I've been distant?"

He nodded.

"I know, Father, and I'm working on it. I do love you. But you have to understand—the decisions you and Mother made on my behalf were extreme. I should have been told at a much younger age. I have decided to tell the truth about this to folks when they ask. I limit the information to 'Mother was married before she married you.' Folks who attended your wedding certainly knew the story. I am just surprised I never heard it in this town after all this time. And with regard to my last name, I tell people that it was easier for me to be known in school as a Graham rather than create confusion for my siblings. I have no intention of dishonoring you or my mother."

"I appreciate that, as would your mother." He exhaled

heavily. "I do miss my daughter. You haven't been home for nearly three days."

"I know. I'll be home as soon as the fever breaks. How is Tiffany?" she asked, redirecting the conversation.

"Most of the time she is doing well, admitting to her shortcomings. There are moments, though, when I think she's ready to just bolt out the door. On the good side, the run-in with the bandits has everyone staying close to home until those men are caught."

"Good. Let her know I miss our sister talks."

"I shall." Her father stood, came over and took her by the hands, helping her up, as well. He pulled her into an embrace. "I love you, sweetheart. Don't ever forget it. I've always tried to do what was best for you."

"Thank you, Daddy. I love you, too."

"You called me 'Daddy'!" John beamed. "I haven't heard that since you were five."

Holly winked. "I love you. I'll keep 'Daddy' for special occasions."

"I like that. Now, please come home and spend the night in your own bed and make certain Chadwick or Ryan escort you."

"I'll try, but don't wait up for me."

John Graham nodded his goodbye and exited the Jarvises' home.

Holly felt more content and at peace than she had since...*when?* As far back as she could remember she had never called John "Daddy." Apparently something had changed when she was five years old.

It was the one piece of the puzzle of her past that she couldn't quite figure out. Her siblings called John "Papa." She had never used that name. Instead she'd called him "Father" since she was five. Why?

A fuzzy image, thick as that horrible night's fog, tried

to form in her mind but vanished as quickly as it had appeared. Holly closed her eyes and tried to retrieve it. Nothing. She groaned and tossed a pillow to the other end of the sofa. "Why can't I remember?"

A few days later, feeling stronger but still incredibly weak, Bryce had had enough. He refused to stay in bed another day. He dressed and worked his way down the stairs. Exhausted, he sat in the parlor and mentally retraced his steps. Going back up again would take even more energy.

"Bryce, what are you doing down here?" His mother scurried to his side.

"I couldn't stay in my room for another minute."

"Very well." She huffed with displeasure. "What can I do for you?"

"I am fine. I just need to rest."

"You are pale as a ghost. I imagine it took a fair amount of effort to dress as well as make it down the stairs in one piece."

Bryce smiled. "Thank you, Mom." He scanned the room. "Where's Holly?"

"Home sleeping, I hope. That girl has been running herself ragged taking care of you and still keeping up her family responsibilities. Thank the good Lord John hired someone to do the cooking and cleaning for the family."

"Who?"

"Widow Sullivan. She's a fine woman and understands what they are going through."

"Yes, I am sure she would be sensitive to their pain."

"May I ask you something, Bryce?"

"Of course." His mother was not one to ask permission to speak. Bryce braced himself for a potentially pointed question.

She wrung the dry towel in her hands. "The night you were attacked, you and Holly had been…"

"Alone at my place, yes. We had a very private conversation about what has transpired between us. A conversation that could not have happened as easily if we were in either one of our families' homes."

"And your honor?"

"Is still intact. We haven't even kissed yet." Bryce thought back to the moment a couple of days ago when they almost had.

"Very well. I trust you and I trust Holly. I just know how temptation can spiral out of control if there are no safeguards in place. And to be in the house you planned on living in as man and wife…"

"I know. And yes, there is temptation, but I will not dishonor Holly or our love for one another. I shall require a short engagement period though."

His mother's smile broadened. "Thank you. I know I am prying but…"

"Relax, Mother. I appreciate your influence in making me a man of integrity. You taught me well."

The front door banged open and Chad barged in, stomping his feet.

"Chadwick Jarvis, what on earth is the matter?"

"Sorry, Mom. I need to speak with… Oh, there you are. Feeling better?"

"Considerably," Bryce replied. "What do you need?"

"Help. There's a problem with the seed order and I am having trouble with the mare. She won't let the stud come near her. We need more stock. At least, I think we do. But if we order more stock there is additional cost in feed. I need you to help me understand what you have in mind here and how you see us making a profit."

Bryce chuckled. "Have a seat. Actually, first go into

my desk and pull out the folder that says 'Ten Year Plan,' upper left drawer."

Chad hustled off to Bryce's office.

"I'll let you two work. Don't push yourself too hard."

"I will be fine, Mother. Besides, I will need to regain my strength to get back up those stairs."

"Chad can always give you a piggyback ride."

"Not on your life," Chad said, coming back with the folder in hand. "I intend to keep my back healthy for a long while."

Bryce chuckled. "Glad to see you have your priorities straight. Let's take a look at the overall picture I have mapped out for the plantation. We are in year three according to this graph." Bryce went on to explain his overall plan and how the slow but steady growth would continue to increase the total profit of the plantation.

"I marvel at your thoroughness, brother. But we are losing money during your third year."

"True. But the profits from the previous year and the larger profit in the fourth year make up for the loss this year."

"But what if we have a bad year, a flood or something like that, and lose the crops? Aren't we risking too much?"

"Not really, look here..." Bryce leaned over, forgetting the pain throbbing in his back. It was good to work again, even if it was limited.

With Bryce's recovery going well, Holly decided to spend more time with her own family. Her absence seemed to have accentuated the loss of their mother for Tiffany and the boys. And on occasion, like today, she even found some time for herself. She took advantage of the peace and quiet to get some sewing done in the sitting room. Until a few days ago she'd been planning on making a tablecloth.

Now she thought in terms of a wedding dress. The lace-work for the dress would take many days and hours. She pulled out her bag of Irish lace, grateful for her mother and grandmother's love for their Irish heritage. First she had to make all the motifs, then the assembly. For this piece she chose simple white flowers.

"Holly, are you home?" The door slammed.

"In the sitting room, Daniel." She placed the motif she was working on in her lap. "Is there a problem?"

He plopped himself down on the chair beside her. "Not really. Calvin plans on hunting again today and I've had my fill of rabbit stew. Can you convince him to change his mind? Please."

"I'll do my best."

"Thank you." Daniel stood.

Holly patted the chair. "Sit, and tell me what's been happening in school."

He obliged. "Not too much. I've had to threaten a few boys, though. Some of the older boys were saying bad things about Tiffany. It's a good thing I'm bigger than most of them, because it seems they've backed off."

"Is it really difficult for Tiff?"

"Hard to say. Seems she gets plenty of attention, good and bad, I suppose. Me, I'm not inclined to ruin a gal's reputation for a simple kiss."

Holly smiled. "You're an honorable young man, Daniel."

"Holly, can I ask you something?"

"Sure."

"Tiff says you never kissed a man, as a boyfriend. She thinks you won't be getting married because you've waited too long. Is she right?"

Holly sighed. She still hadn't gotten through to Tiffany. "No, she isn't right. I believe my husband will be pleased that I waited for him."

"Are you and Bryce going to get married?"

"I don't know. I like him and he likes me, but with Momma's passing I..." She paused.

"I understand. Life is so different without Momma. The house feels different. I'm different. Everything has changed and yet everything is still the same. It's like the colors aren't as bright and the music isn't as clear or beautiful."

"You're absolutely right. I know I am doing better now than the first months after Mother passed away. I felt numb."

"Yeah. Papa cries at night. He doesn't think anyone can hear him. But my room is above his and, well, the sound carries. He cries out to God for strength and help—sometimes about you. You hurt him, Holly."

"I know. I didn't mean to. He misses Momma."

"It was a mistake that you were lied to all those years. But Papa loves you."

"And I love him, too. He will always be my father. He and I had a good talk the other day."

"Yeah, I figured that. I heard him thank God for giving you back to him. Losing Momma is not the same for us as it is for Papa. He lost his best friend. Can you imagine losing Bryce?"

"Unfortunately, I can. I'm very thankful he's still here."

"Yeah, I suppose you can. Have they caught the men who ambushed you?"

"Not yet. We didn't get a good look at the others, only the one man who jumped out in front of us."

The door banged open and Calvin announced, "I'm home."

"Calvin," Holly called, "would you come here, please?"

"Sure." She heard a plop of his books on the floor followed by the patter of his shoes. He came in and eyed Daniel. "You told her, didn't you?"

Holly gave Daniel a nod. "Would you excuse us for a moment, please?"

"Sure." Daniel stood and offered his seat to Calvin.

Daniel left, and Holly picked up the sewing again.

"Why the need to hunt so often, Calvin?"

"Because I like it." Calvin grinned.

"What is it about hunting that you enjoy so much?"

"I'm helping the family by being a provider, like Momma said. She said I was a good hunter and provider."

"Ah, I think I understand. Do you know that Momma was pleased by many of the things you did? Like how well you do in your schooling and how well you clean your room."

"I know. But she said I was a really good hunter."

"Yes, but by hunting so often you aren't doing as well in school. You are forgetting to do your homework. Your teacher, Miss Clark, sent a note home with Riley."

Calvin slumped in the chair. "I just forgot."

"Would it please Momma to see you neglecting your studies because you want to go hunting every other day?"

"No, I suppose not."

"How about if you plan a hunting trip once a month? Maybe Papa can go with you and you can track down some turkey or deer."

"Do you think Papa would wanna come?"

"Yes, I think he would."

Calvin shook his head as if unsure. "So I shouldn't go hunting as much so I can do my schoolwork?"

"See, that's the smart boy that Momma was so proud of. Yes, I think you should do as good a job with your schoolwork as you do hunting. We both know that's what Momma would want, don't we?"

He jumped off his seat. "All right. Can I ask Papa about hunting?"

"Sure, as soon as he gets home."

Calvin ran out of the room and she heard his feet scurry up the stairs. Riley leaned against the door casing. "You're good."

Holly laughed. "And how are you today?"

"Learning something new every day. So, what are you working on?"

"Some Irish lace."

"Are you half Irish like us or full Irish?"

"My father is Scottish, so I'm that mix."

"You know, it is kinda strange having you be a half sister not a whole one."

Holly stretched out her arms and gave herself an exaggerated exam. "I appear to be whole."

Riley laughed. "You know what I mean."

"I do, but has it really changed anything? I'm your older sister. I've always been your older sister and always will be. So what's different?"

"Hmm." Riley pondered for a moment. "I reckon you're right. Only thing that is different is your last name."

"Which apparently it always was. We just didn't know it."

"Who can explain that?"

"I simply tell people that it made it easier for school and my siblings that I went by the same last name as the rest of the family."

"Oh, I like that. You know all the kids at school are talkin' about it. Now I have something to say to 'em."

"I'll be the big story until something else comes along."

"Well, your last name isn't the big story right now. Now everybody's talkin' about you, Bryce and the bandits. Were you scared?"

Chapter 12

"It's been a long three weeks, hasn't it?"

"Holly!" Bryce dropped the bundle he'd just picked up back in the wagon. "It is so good to see you. It seems like ages, and it has only been two days. How is your family?"

"We're doing well." Her green eyes sparkled in the sunlight. He wished he could lift her in his arms from the gig, twirl her around and kiss her soundly on the lips. But there would come a time and a place for that. Today was not that day.

"I thought I'd give you a hand moving back into your own home. I also brought dinner. We just won't be making it a late night this time."

Bryce chuckled then grabbed his back and grimaced. "No, I agree, that would not be a good idea."

"How are you?" She climbed out of the gig.

"Better, much better. I need to keep busy, though. With

all the attention I am getting at my parents' house I shall never regain my strength."

"I'd like to help if I can. Along with the dinner, I brought some fresh-baked bread."

"Dinner probably wouldn't be wise. I would like you to leave with plenty of daylight still in the sky."

"Agreed. I cannot believe the sheriff hasn't caught them yet."

"Nor I." Bryce grabbed the bundle again and headed for the house.

Holly followed, taking the dinner and his valise. "I've been having several conversations with my brothers about Mother's passing. They are doing much better. I did let my father know that Daniel can hear his late-night prayers."

"I am certain it was an embarrassment for your father, but I wonder if hearing his prayers has helped Daniel understand his own loss."

"As well as mine."

Bryce took the key from his pocket and opened the door. A blast of stale air assaulted him. "I need to open some windows."

"I'll be happy to do that while you unload the rest of your stuff. How'd you end up with so many packages?"

"Mother. She has decided I need a few more items to make my house cozier. Truthfully, I am not even going to unpack them. I received word from the Turners that they want to purchase the house."

"Oh." Holly sighed.

"Holly...honey, do you want this house?"

"I don't know. It's gorgeous, and I could be very comfortable here. But you and I haven't even started the courtship process. It will be a year before we marry."

Bryce placed his bundle on the kitchen counter and took

her in his arms. "It doesn't have to be a long engagement. We could marry today if you would like."

Holly let out a nervous laugh and closed her eyes. "Bryce, I love you, I really do. But today would be too soon. I am no different than all the other girls when it comes to wanting to walk down the aisle in church with all our friends and family in attendance. And when I say 'all,' I am including my family from Tennessee. Besides, you haven't even asked me to marry you."

Bryce brushed the red locks of hair sweeping across her face behind her ear. "Today is too soon. I am not healthy enough to carry you across the threshold."

"I am looking forward to that day."

"Good." He released his hold and stepped back. "Now that today is settled, how about next week?"

She swatted his arm. "I think we're talking a few months at the very least. I know I am doing a lot better but I still have some nagging, unsettling questions about the past."

"Have you talked with your fathers about them?"

"I've written a letter to Emmett and I am hoping to hear from him soon. I doubt he'll be able to help me, but you never know. I haven't had the heart to mention it to John. Our relationship is better, although it's not the same since Mother died."

"Come here." He pulled her into his chest and held her. He couldn't give her the answers she sought. He could, however, give her love and comfort and security. He kissed the top of her head and felt her breathing calm. "Holly?"

"Hmm?" she whispered.

"Do you know that I love you?"

She eased back from his embrace and looked into his eyes. "Yes."

"And do you know without a doubt that you love me,

and that this love is forever, to be shared only between you and me?"

"Oh, yes, Bryce, I do, without one doubt. I'm uncertain about when I'll be able to give you my love completely. There's still a part of me that is... I was going to say angry, but angry isn't the right word. Perhaps frustrated better describes what I'm feeling. It's a much smaller problem than the day I first learned everything, but it is still there."

He caressed her cheek with his fingers. "Then dear, sweet Holly, I will not kiss you, not yet."

Holly groaned. "But I want to kiss you."

"And I, you. But I made a promise to you in the barn and I intend to keep it. We will continue to pray and trust the Lord to remove the barrier first."

Holly stepped back and turned away from him. He knew it wasn't rejection, yet a near-physical pain seared his heart. Every impulse urged him to swoop her into his arms and chase away her fears and frustrations with a kiss. But Holly needed him to honor his word. He needed to honor his word. She deserved a clean slate without doubts, lies or half admissions to the truth. He could wait. She'd come so far. He stepped toward her and placed his hands on her shoulders. She leaned into him. "Holly, sweetheart. I will be patient. You can depend on me."

She bowed her head. "I know."

He kissed the top of her head again. "Soon, my love. Soon." Then, with every ounce of his strength and moral convictions, he released her and went outside to gather the rest of his belongings. "Thank you, Lord, for the strength. Please give me more," he prayed as he walked across the yard to the wagon.

"Bryce Jarvis, is that you? It's me, Whit Butterfield."

Bryce turned to his left. "Whit, what are you doing here?"

"Word is you had a run-in with some fellas a while back and I've been looking into it. May we talk?"

"Sure, come inside." Bryce paused. "Holly is in the house."

"I've made my peace with the Graham family."

Bryce let out a pent-up breath. "And I need to apologize to you, as well. I was out of line at the cemetery."

"Yes, sir, but you didn't say anything I didn't already feel."

"No, Whit, I was wrong. I should have run after you that day and apologized right then and there. I can be terribly stubborn sometimes. Forgive me."

Whit raised a hand. "It's forgotten. Now, you wanna hear what I learned?"

"Absolutely. Let's go inside." Bryce grabbed one of the bundles and Whit the other.

"Holly, we have a guest."

Holly turned from the kitchen sink. Her smile faded once she recognized who it was. "Hello, Mr. Butterfield."

"Hello, Miss Graham."

Bryce noticed Holly didn't correct him.

"What did you want to tell me, Whit?"

"What can you remember about the man you tied up?" Whit leaned against the counter.

"You're investigating Bryce's shooting?"

"Yes. I'm not a deputy sheriff or anything like that. But I've heard some mumblings on the street and, well, I thought if I knew what one of the guys looked like I might be able to give the sheriff some helpful information."

"Coffee? Tea?" Holly asked.

"Water, thank you," Whit answered.

"Bryce?"

"Tea, thanks. I don't think I am up for coffee at this hour. Whit, please have a seat." Bryce motioned toward the kitchen table. "I am afraid I don't have much in the way of furnishings."

"Makes no never mind to me. I heard some fellas gettin' all worked up about not being able to make any money on the streets at night lately. They mentioned your incident and how folks were staying off the roads at night or coming out heavily guarded."

"Just about everyone is talking about that," Holly offered.

"Except for the part about them not being able to make money. Who makes money off of folks using the streets at night?" Whit asked.

Holly nodded.

"Agreed," Bryce said as he eased himself down in the chair. The wound was tender and the short move from his parents' plantation to his house had irritated it. "Did you get a good look at them?" he asked Whit.

"Not too good. Besides, I wanted to talk with you first. There was one guy with brown, roughly cut hair a bit long on the collar. The other wore a dark hat so I couldn't see much. I didn't face them. They were behind me and I was trying to listen without appearin' to be listenin', if ya know what I mean."

"Yes." Holly and Bryce echoed one another.

"It was foggy, and I could barely see. But the man who came out of the bushes stepped into a sudden patch of light," Holly told him. "He had a dark beard, an unkempt appearance. He wore old overalls and heavy work boots. And his partner called him Tom."

"When I tied him up," Bryce added, "he seemed thinner than he appeared standing in front of me. I gave him a good kick on the side of the head. I don't know if I broke the skin or not but he must have had at least a bruise for a while."

"More than likely it would be gone by now. Been close to three weeks, ain't it?"

"Yes," Bryce admitted.

Holly gazed out the window. "The sun is starting to set. I better head on home."

"Be happy to provide an escort, Miss Graham. No sense anyone else getting hurt."

Holly paused. Bryce watched her eyes dart back and forth between Whit and himself. "I'd appreciate that."

Bryce nodded in agreement. He should be the one to escort Holly, but how could he defend her if necessary? "Thanks, Whit," he said. "I appreciate it."

"Be an honor."

Holly placed a hand on Bryce's shoulder and squeezed. "Do you need me to change the bandage before I leave?"

"Probably should check and see. I didn't feel any bleeding, but you never can tell." Bryce rose from the chair and lifted his shirt.

"It's clean, no bleeding." Holly smiled. "I'll see you tomorrow."

"Tomorrow."

Whit nodded. "I'll take good care of her. You have my word, Bryce."

Whit extended his hand and Bryce shook it. "Thanks, again. You be careful with your investigating, and as soon as you know anything, tell the sheriff."

"Don't worry none. My wife and children are important to me. Things been tight since the accident and I care for my own."

In that moment Bryce realized just how difficult life had gotten for Whit Butterfield and his family. In truth, the accident was no one's fault. Allison Graham had slipped and fallen in front of Whit's wagon. No one could have stopped in time. "Dear God," Bryce silently prayed, "forgive me for my anger against Whit. Supply their needs and give him and Holly safe passage on the road tonight."

"Good morning, Bryce." Holly loved the startled expression on his face. He was so handsome, even in his disheveled state. Today she'd dressed in a whimsical style—a white blouse with tiny lilac flowers and a deep purple skirt. She did love purple.

"Holly, what are you doing here so early? You look wonderful."

"Thank you. I wanted to finish our conversation."

Bryce placed the mug of coffee down on the table.

"May I have a cup?"

"Certainly." He jumped up and winced.

"Stay there, I'll take care of it. I brought some fresh milk and eggs from home. Would you like me to fix some breakfast?"

His smile warmed her. "Thank you, but I have already eaten." He eased back into his chair. "So what do we have to discuss?"

"The house."

Bryce sat straight up.

"I know why you purchased it. I'm wondering if it holds bitter memories for you."

"Nothing that cannot be erased. Holly, I don't mind keeping the house, or we can purchase another home. It is up to you."

Holly worried her lower lip. "I am undecided. Because Jessie and her husband are interested, I thought perhaps we should discuss this." She poured some cream and a rounded teaspoon of sugar into her coffee cup and stirred.

"I can tell the Turners that my fiancée is having second thoughts about the house." He winked.

Holly giggled and brought her coffee to the table. "I'm not your fiancée."

"You will be." Bryce reached across the table and took her hand.

Her fingers relaxed within his palm. "Why can't I just say yes?"

"Because you are still healing. Honey, I understand you need more time. This may not be the right house for us. On the other hand, I don't mind living in it by myself until we are married. But I don't want to do anything that will make you afraid of committing to me. And if keeping the house right now feels like undue pressure, then I will sell it. I will make a good profit, which I can use toward the purchase of another home. I have investigated several possible houses. Perhaps I should show them to you and you can help me decide which has the most potential."

"That sounds like fun."

"Great, we shall go on the great house hunt. Some of these houses I have looked at have great structure but the interior has come upon bad times. All repairable but not pretty, like this place was. All the floors needed to be sanded, stained and polished. They are the original floor-boards, just…"

"Refinished," she supplied for him.

"Precisely. There is something else you should know about me and my future plans."

"What's that?"

"I like investing in real estate. From time to time I will want to purchase and resell property. I am fairly certain I don't want to deal with tenants. I have seen what they can do to a property. Buying and selling turns investment into profit. In our case, it will provide the finances we need to travel abroad. By the way, are you interested in honey-mooning in Venice?"

"Does a cow give milk?"

Bryce laughed, gripping his side to ease the pain.

"Sorry." Holly sipped her coffee. "I have a question for you."

He leaned back in his chair. "I am at your command."

"I am confused by your desire to live inside the city limits. For years you've talked about the land, raising crops, livestock… You cannot do that in the city. Wouldn't you rather live on a small farm or plantation?"

"I do like working with my hands. And Father needs me to run the plantation, so I will always be working the land."

"I guess, I just thought you would want a piece of land that was your own."

"You are forgetting I am the oldest son. The greater land share goes to me after my father passes. What are you asking, Holly?"

"I don't see you content living in the city, and I don't see myself—or you for that matter—wanting to move every six months to a year because you've purchased and sold another house. I mean, I don't mind… Oh, I don't know what I mean. I guess it doesn't sound like a stable environment for children."

"Children, hmm? So you are thinking about having children with me one day?" He wiggled his eyebrows.

Holly groaned. "Of course we'll have children, if the Lord blesses us with them. Can we stay to the topic at hand, please?"

Bryce nodded and leaned forward on his forearms, cupping his coffee mug with both hands. "Here is my plan at a quick glance. If I purchase a house, improve it and sell it again, I will make a profit. The goal is to eventually purchase a house and owe nothing on it at the time of purchase. I am hoping to achieve this in five years. And should we marry and be blessed with children early on, they would be young enough to move into our final home and be none the wiser with regard to all the moves."

"So, you have a goal. Of course you have a goal. You've always had goals and plans. I was just seeing an endless future of packing and unpacking again and again."

"No, I wouldn't put you through that." Bryce shook his head.

"I have another question about us."

"At your service, my lady." Bryce pretended to take a hat from his head and give a slight bow.

"How long are you really willing to wait for me? My problem is, I don't know what this block in my heart is or how long it will take before it is gone. I know there's more going on than just this memory I cannot retrieve. I cannot promise to fully love you as long as my heart is still so confused."

He held out both his hands palm up and waited. Holly tentatively placed her left hand in his right and her right in his left. He curled his thumbs over the tops of her fingers and gently caressed them. "Honey, it has only been three months since your mother died and your world was turned upside down. From what you said to me, whatever is blocking your heart is down to a fraction of what it was before. You are no longer numb. You feel joy and pain. You cry easily. Give it time. I am certain we will get to the point where that area of your heart will be completely healed.

"Ask yourself this. What are you feeling when we hold hands like this?"

Comfort, peace, completeness came to mind at once. Her thoughts then burrowed deeper down, taking her into distant, indistinct memories where she could sense that strange place in her heart that refused to feel anything. No, that was not quite accurate. It felt hard, cold and without emotion. "It's still there."

"Yes, but is it as large as it was last week?"

"No, it is smaller."

He released her hands. "That's my girl. That's what I was looking for."

Holly smiled and focused on Bryce's honey-brown eyes. She'd never met another with eyes that warm shade, apart from his mother. She could get lost in those eyes. "I see your point. You are counting on hope."

"And you. You are a strong woman, Holly. I know you'll grow through this. Not only will you be a stronger and richer person afterward but so will I be. I find strength in you, too. You encourage me to be more than I am. I could simply stay at the plantation, do my father's bidding and inherit it, but I want to make my own way in the world. I am not seeking immeasurable wealth."

"This seems so strange. We're talking about our future lives together and we aren't officially courting yet." Holly closed her eyes and bowed her head. "I love you, Bryce. I truly do. I wish I could give you all of my heart. But…" She lifted her head and focused on his wonderful eyes. "Goodness, I want to kiss you."

Bryce beamed. "That's a good place to start. Relax, Holly. We will get through this. We just have to give you more time to heal and recover that memory."

"What if I never do?"

"I believe you will. You're already seeing shadows of an event. Give it time."

Holly finished off her coffee. She wanted a life with Bryce. She always had. "I've never been good with patience."

Bryce stood. "Yes, I am well aware of that." He winked. "Whereas I have always been more methodical, except when it came to you. You seemed to get me into trouble."

Holly giggled. "Were you planning on selling this house as part of your five-year plan for a debt-free home?"

"Yes."

"Then let's sell it. I would love to go house hunting with you today."

He placed his mug on the counter next to the sink and came up beside her, helping her from her seat and engulfing her in a bear hug that lifted her off her feet.

"Bryce Jarvis, put me down." She laughed. "You'll re-open that wound."

"Nah, you don't weigh much." He eased her back to the floor. "Let me get the buggy and we shall be on our way."

Chapter 13

"I think the house on West Charlton Street next to Pulaski Square doesn't have enough of a yard to interest a family," Holly said as she climbed back into the buggy. "The one on East Taylor Street, however, has a good yard but the house seems too small." She sat on the bench seat. "That's probably not very helpful. I am not real good at this. Sorry, Bryce."

Bryce couldn't help but smile. "No, you are great. I noticed the same issues."

"Really?"

"Yes." The buggy creaked as he climbed up and took the reins. "The thing about investing in real estate is that you have to choose wisely. You not only have to look at location but also the potential a house would offer to particular types of clients. How much it will cost to improve the house and still bring a high enough profit margin to

warrant investment of time is another major consideration."
He paused. "I hope I am not boring you with details."

"You are not boring me at all."

The smile on her face lifted his spirits. "Good. I have
another location a little farther out of town. The listing
price seems reasonable. It's on East Anderson halfway
between Forsythe Park and Evergreen. The only concern
I have is that the house isn't all that old, whereas the two
we've already looked at were built last century. This one
is much newer, about twenty years old."

"Does the age of the house make much difference?"

"Different materials were used when they built the older
homes. Today we use much more gypsum in our horsehair plaster."

"Do you really put horsehair in the plaster?"

"Yes. It helps give the plaster more strength and binds
well to the lathe work behind it."

"Are you certain you want to run plantations? You're
sounding more and more like real estate's in your blood."

Bryce chuckled and kept on driving. "Truthfully, I don't
like working with horsehair plaster. It itches. However, if I
want to make a large profit I have to be willing to do most,
if not all, of the work. What I really love is working with
livestock, especially breeding horses."

A strange grin spread over Holly's face.

"What?"

"That's what my father does in Tennessee."

"Really? Can you tell me about his ranch?"

"It's very large, with several barns for different purposes. There is a large enclosed arena where they train the
horses. It's not what you would consider classic architecture, but it is a very interesting building. I was surprised
to see just how large a working ranch it was. He also raises
some cattle and sheep, but the primary stock is the horses."

"I would love to see his ranch sometime. You never told me about your other family. How do you feel about them? What are they like?"

Bryce drove the buggy at a leisurely pace while Holly regaled him with stories about her Tennessee stepmother, two stepsisters and stepbrothers. He could have been through by now but being with Holly far outweighed any issue with time.

"That's quite a family. Between the Landers and Grahams you have three sisters and five brothers. What are you going to do for Christmas?"

"I haven't thought that far ahead. I cannot see myself celebrating the holiday anywhere but here. I will need to plan ahead for my Tennessee family. A shipment of oranges and grapefruit would add to their holiday celebrations." Holly knitted her eyebrows.

"I'll have to think about that. I cannot believe I am thinking about Christmas and it is only October."

"Yes, but with regard to shipping, you always need to get items out early. Unless you are planning a trip and can take them with you. I wouldn't mind escorting you to Tennessee. Perhaps as your husband."

Holly smiled. "That would be nice." Then just as quickly her shoulders slumped and her complexion changed.

"Holly?"

He watched her eyelids close. He prayed for the Lord to give her peace and to break down the final barrier in her heart.

Slowly she opened her eyes and placed her hand on his forearm. "I do so want to marry you. When we are alone like this, just talking, I feel so close to you and there is nothing stopping me from loving you. Then the moment I think that, I feel that…that… Oh, what do I call it? It's like a harness on my heart holding me back. I hate it. And I simply don't know how to get rid of it."

"Give it time, honey. Give it over to God and eventually He will remove it."

"I'm still mad at God when I think about Mother's accident. He could have prevented it and chose not to. Then again, I wouldn't know my real father and his family if she hadn't died. It's so confusing. John admitted he was the primary one preventing me from knowing until I was twenty-one and that he kept the suitors away. Apparently there have been quite a few seeking my affections."

Bryce stiffened. "But you are not interested—"

She cut him off. "No, of course I'm not interested in seeking any other man's affections."

"That is a relief. I am not fit enough to duel at the moment."

Holly laughed. "My knight in shining armor."

"I was thinking more along the line of the Three Musketeers, but I could be one of King Arthur's Knights." Bryce turned the buggy into the driveway. "Here we are. What do you think?"

"First impression is nice. It has a lovely yard and wraparound front porch."

"And I like the carriage house with its second floor. Let's check out the interior." Bryce watched the satisfied smile bloom on Holly's cheek. He scanned the area, rich with vacant land this far out of the city. A field large enough for a horse to graze stretched away from the right of the house. Patches of grass divided the two-lane dirt road in the front. It wasn't as large as some of the streets inside the city but allowed room enough for two carriages to pass one another on opposite sides without either having to give way. Bryce searched the lines of the house. The roof ridge didn't sag. The sides and corners stood straight and plumb. "I wonder why they put the house on the market."

Bryce stepped down and circled the buggy to offer her assistance. She grasped his hand with her delicate fingers and glided down. She had the grace and poise of any well-trained Southern belle, yet this was his Holly, rough and tumble, who played hard and swept him off his feet. "I love you," he whispered.

Their gazes locked for a moment then she replied, "I love you, too." She glanced away as soon as the words left her lips.

Patience, Bryce, you can do this. Give her the time you promised her earlier. "Shall we?"

She snapped back and refocused on him. He smiled but said not a word. Yes, patience would win. She placed her hand in the crook of his elbow. "Yes, let's go."

Holly stepped into the backyard with Bryce. The house had great potential, very little appeared wrong with it. All it needed was some fresh wallpaper, paint and a good scrubbing. "You said this house has a low price on it? There doesn't seem to be much in disrepair."

"Yes, and that concerns me, too. Why the price? What are we not seeing?" Bryce stepped farther into the backyard.

"Stop!" Holly screamed.

Bryce jumped. Holly started to shake.

"What's the matter?"

He had her in his embrace before she could get a word out. "I cannot explain it. But I think there's a pit or something just about where you were going to step."

"What? Have you been here before?"

"No. Not that I remember. I…I cannot explain it. I saw

you heading over there and this image of the earth swallowing you whole came into mind."

"Let me check." Bryce released her. He grabbed an old rake he found on the ground and started poking the earth in front of him with the handle. "The ground seems solid."

Holly couldn't shake the image. She wrapped her arms around herself.

Bryce continued his exploration. He turned and looked at her. "Holly, are you all right?"

She nodded. What had she seen? Her mind flashed back to darkness, a tunnel, the dim light of the sky overhead, then nothing. She felt cold. Her legs gave out and she crumpled to the ground.

"Holly? Holly?" Bryce's voice floated in her consciousness. She was in his arms. No, she was on his lap. They were on the ground together. He held her tight and rocked back and forth. "Shh, honey, everything is going to be all right."

"This has never happened to me before," she confessed. His sweet masculine scent enveloped her as she nestled her head on his shoulder. "I saw a tunnel or pit or something. It was dark…cold…wet, and there was only a pinhole of a sky up above me. I was terrified."

"Do you think this is a real memory? Maybe a nightmare?"

"I don't know. Goodness, what is happening to me, Bryce? Am I losing my mind?"

"No, I don't believe you are losing your mind. Something in this yard or house triggered a memory of some sort. The way you reacted reminded me of reactions I saw in some of my father's friends who fought in the war."

Holly took in a deep breath and eased it out slowly. The fear that had taken over her body now changed to desire. She traced Bryce's neck with her finger.

"Holly, honey, stop, please." He shifted her from his lap to the ground beside him.

"Sorry." She could feel the heat build on her cheeks. She brought her knees up to her chin and wrapped her arms around her legs. "What's wrong with me? All of a sudden I am overcome by strange memories, or imagined ones, and lose complete control and simply react. Then I relax in your arms and…and… Well, you know."

"Shh, everything will be fine. Let's talk about what you saw."

"It was more felt than saw. But as you stepped into the yard I saw blackness, almost complete blackness. Then I looked up and saw the blue sky as this tiny circle of light. I felt myself fall on wet and cold ground, like I was stuck in a pit."

"Or a well, perhaps?" Bryce suggested. "Is it possible that you might have fallen into a well when you were a small child?"

"Anything is possible, although I have no memory of it. And I don't recall ever being at this house before. Yet there is something familiar about this yard. I cannot place it. But there is something."

Bryce got up from the ground and extended his hand to her. "Come, let us explore the yard together. We will keep checking the ground before we step forward, just in case your memory happened here."

"But why would it? I don't think my grandparents or my mother ever lived here. When she returned from Tennessee, she and I moved in with my grandparents, according to my fathers."

"What you remember may not have actually happened here, but something in this yard sparked that memory. Perhaps if we continue walking around, some other pieces will surface."

"Sounds wonderful," she quipped.

Bryce stopped and had her face him. He brushed the strands of hair from her face. "If this is too hard we can stop…"

"If I can retrieve more memories maybe we can figure out what the hardness is in my heart and get on with our lives."

"I would not have been as direct, but I agree."

Holly closed her eyes and tried to refocus on the traces of the memory she'd seen. "I cannot see anything."

"Relax. Let us walk the property. You were on the back stairs when you hollered out to me. Let us start there. I will walk ahead of you like before. Perhaps it will ignite the images again."

"All right." Holly faced the house and paused. She looked up at the second-floor window below the peak. There appeared to be a silhouette of an eagle with outstretched wings on the paint. Holly stepped back to get a better view. She'd seen those eagle images before. They represented the Revolutionary War. "Bryce," she said, pointing, "do you see what appears to be where an eagle plaque once hung up there?"

"Yes, why?"

"No reason, I guess. It seems familiar. Of course, many homes have them over their doorways." Holly shook her head, went back to the steps and turned to face the backyard. Bryce hustled out in front of her. "It's not happening this time."

"That is fine. Come, let us finish checking out the place." He held out his hand and she joined him for a leisurely walk around the yard. Nothing came; no fear, no sudden memories. Instead she found herself getting caught up in Bryce's analysis of the property.

"So, what do you think?" Holly asked.

"I am curious about the price. It seems low for a house in such good repair. Granted, there is some work needed on the interior, but all simple fixes. It is a bit odd. But I will investigate some more. It may be that the children inherited the place and don't live in the area. They may simply want to sell it quickly."

"I suppose. But they took out the furnishings. And who took an ax to that wall in there. What do you suppose happened?"

"It is a curiosity but an easy repair."

"It seems odd. On the other hand, I'm still a bit shaky from whatever that was I remembered earlier. It seemed so real. I was certain you would step into a pit of some sort."

"You should ask your father if he recalls a time when you fell into a well."

"You are right, a well sounds as plausible as anything else."

"You mentioned it was narrow and damp."

Holly nodded. The flash of a bucket coming down at her flitted through her mind. She closed her eyes and replayed the memory. It had to be a memory. What else could explain it? Falling down an old well wasn't unheard of. She thought of the faded scar on her right ankle. Had that injury occurred during the same event?

"Bryce, I think I did fall down a well. I was young, very young. There's a scar on my right ankle. It's been there for as long as I can remember. I must have fallen down a well and injured my ankle. I remember a bucket being lowered to me…but it wasn't really a bucket. I don't know…it's just bits and pieces."

Bryce smiled. "The memory will come. Unless you want to stay longer, I think it is time for us to head back."

"Father will begin to wonder what I am doing. I did say

I was going to give you a hand but he doesn't like me gone for that long. He can be a bit controlling."

Bryce chuckled. "No comment. Shall we?" He held out his elbow and escorted her back to their buggy.

"So what's the process now, if you decide to buy this house?"

"First, I will want to discuss it with you because you and I will probably live in this house together for a while before we purchase the next one. After that, I make an offer. Normally, you offer less than they wish to sell it for, factoring in what it will take to repair the house. The folks selling the house tend to ask more than what the true value is. However, in this case, I will want to inspect it more closely before I put in a bid. I want to check for termite damage. I did not see any, but that could be the reason the price is so low. I probably won't dicker much on this price. I will check the survey records and the reasons the house is up for sale. How many people have owned the house? How long since someone has lived in it? Were they tenants or owners? Those kinds of questions will help me determine whether this is a sound investment or not."

"So, if the house has had a lot of owners, why is the house always up for sale and will that hurt your chances of selling it for a profit."

"Precisely."

Bryce helped her into the buggy. He guided the horse and carriage back onto the street and headed toward his house.

"What is the asking price, if you don't mind? I mean, Father never spoke of financial matters with Mother, so I understand if you don't want to involve me."

"I have no problem speaking of our finances with you. The house is on the market for seven thousand. It is easily worth ten and a half, possibly up to twelve. It all depends on the amount of land."

"And what about your current house?"

"I purchased it for sixty-five hundred. I spent two thousand in materials and another thousand in labor, which means I have to sell for over eleven to make a real profit. I am asking twelve. I won't go below eleven and a half. The location is ideal. The carriage house and the corner lot all help with the value."

"Jessie and Jeff Turner are willing to pay the twelve?"

"No, he wants it for eleven. I cannot go that low. I can wait for a while to see if I have any other buyers. I would like to help the Turners out, but I have to be firm on the profit margin."

Holly's back stiffened. "You know they are with child?"

Bryce glanced at her then back at the road. "Honey, I am sorry. This has to be about business. I cannot get personal with regard to business. I will never make a profit if I don't keep that focus."

"Forgive me if I'm not understanding correctly, but if you sell the house for eleven you still make a profit of fifteen hundred, don't you?"

"Yes but…"

"You have a goal of earning at least two thousand off of the purchase of each house?"

"Well, yes. Five houses, five years, a profit of two thousand and we can purchase a ten-thousand-dollar home with no mortgage."

Holly nodded. "I understand." *The business side,* she said to herself. *But are you missing the human side?* she wondered.

"Thank you, it means a lot to me to have your favor."

Holly groaned. "I am sorry, Bryce. I understand. I don't necessarily agree with you."

"Oh." They continued the rest of the trip in silence.

She'd done it again. Opened her mouth and inserted her foot. He'd said he wanted her input. But she did have a tendency for saying things straight and to the point. "I'm sorry."

"No, don't be. Learning to work with each other in matters like this will help us deal with the bigger issues that will come our way while raising children. That will be tougher than any financial matter. You have given me something to think about and I will.

"Honey, I was not angry with you. I was analyzing your point. You know that I always have a plan, a goal. Am I inflexible? Do I need to be more flexible with these kinds of matters? Or do I need to stay firm in order to make the profit necessary to achieve our goals? These are just a few of the questions that were going on in my mind."

Relief washed over her. "Then let me add one more question into the mix. I've been struggling with God ever since Mother's death. And yet when you told me your plan for our future and your financial desire to purchase a house outright in five years, where was God in that decision? Shouldn't you consult Him, too?"

Bryce sighed. "You are right. I need to give this matter further thought...and prayer. However, I have other business to attend to. I shall drive the buggy back to my place and get my horse. You can go on to your home from there."

Holly smiled. "I would like that."

Bryce pulled the buggy to the side of the street and dashed off into his carriage house.

And what about you, Miss Holly Elizabeth Landers? Where is God in the decisions you've been making about your future?

Chapter 14

Bryce scanned the sides of the road. Whit Butterfield should be heading this way soon. In an effort to help Whit and his family out, he'd hired him to do some work on the plantation.

"Are you all right?" Holly asked.

"Fine," he lied. "I am remembering the last time we took a ride along this road."

"Ah. Well, the rifle is loaded and I see you have your revolver on."

He grinned. "We need to be careful until those guys are caught."

"Agreed. I need to confess something to you. My challenging you with regard to the Lord in your decision-making is because I'm having trouble doing the same."

He placed both reins in his left hand and put his right hand on top of her folded ones. "I know you are struggling with your mother's death and God's allowance."

Holly nodded.

"But you were right. I can get caught up in my business agenda and not seek God's favor. Tell me how you are feeling about God and the death of your mother?"

"I know in my head and in God's Word that everyone has a time to live and a time to die. It's appointed by God. However, it doesn't seem fair when you consider what others go through. Look at me, for example. All the pain of the loss of my mother, the supposed death of my father, who I didn't know then… I don't know… I guess I'm just frustrated with the fact that I cannot ask my mother questions, compounded by the very real hurt of not being able to speak with her again about anything. She won't be there when I get married. She won't be there for my children. They won't have a grandmother. Well, they will with your mom, of course, but…"

"They will have three grandfathers and two grandmothers." Bryce smiled.

Holly paused. "I suppose that is so. But they won't know my mom, and she was a special woman."

"Yes, your mother will never get to love our children like other grandmothers do. However, they will know your mom through you and me. We will tell them stories about her, share some of the things she has done. They may not know her here and now but they will know her."

Holly laid her head on his shoulder. "You're right. They will have an opportunity to know her. Father will certainly tell stories, and so will their aunt Tiffany and their uncles."

"And do not forget my brothers and sister. Together, the entire lot of us will continue her legacy. And what about your fancy Irish lacework that you learned from your mother? If we have a daughter, I suspect you will be teaching her as your mother taught you and your mom's mom taught her."

"That's true."

Bryce slipped his hand off of Holly's.

"Problem?" she whispered.

"Stay alert," he whispered back. "It is probably just an animal but I want to be careful."

She reached into her purse. "I have a gun, too," she whispered.

A man jumped out of the bushes with his rifle aimed at Bryce. "Well, looky here, you survived. And aren't we all cuddly and romantic." Two men jumped out from the opposite side of the road.

"What do you want?" Bryce asked.

"Your money and your horses. And this time we'll take the girl, as well."

Holly sat ramrod-straight.

"I don't believe you want to do that," Bryce warned.

"Oh, no? And why is that?" The lead bandit spat to the ground.

"Because in just about a minute there will be several other men coming up alongside us."

"Sure, and the Pope ain't catholic, either."

Bryce toed the rifle from the footboard and positioned it for a quick release. Holly's hand slid deeper into her bag. His right hand curled around the handle of his Colt 45. "I will give you the horses. I will even give you the buggy. But you cannot have the lady."

An evil laugh whistled through the man's teeth. "And who's going to stop me? You?"

"You ain't recovered from the last bullet I planted in ya." One of the men from the side snickered.

The cocking of a gun from behind them echoed through the woods.

"The man said scram." Whit Butterfield's voice boomed. "Me and my own say drop your weapons."

Bryce pulled out his Colt. Holly did the same. The three men dropped their weapons.

"Tie 'em up, Bryce. I'll keep an eye on them. If they so much as blink I'll put a bullet through 'em." Bryce jumped down and left his .45 on the buggy's bench seat. He walked back to his horse and cut a length of rope hanging off the saddle horn.

He first tied the man who had admitted to shooting him. Then he moved on to the lead man who had made the initial contact.

Chad approached as he was finishing the knot around the second man. "Need a hand, big brother?"

"Sure, get that one."

"Will do." Chad dismounted and grabbed a leather strap from his saddle. "These the same guys?"

"Yes." Bryce glanced back at Holly. She was pale but breathing well. "Whit, are you and Chad up to bringing these guys in? Tell the sheriff I will come by this evening and write out my statement."

"Be my pleasure," Whit said.

"And here I was planning on taking a day off. I suppose I can help with this," Chad teased.

"I know, I am such a burden sometimes."

"And don't you forget it. You still owe me for all those chores I did for you while you were nursing that gunshot wound. You'd think you were dying or something."

Bryce laughed. "Or something." He turned back to Holly. Her mouth gaped open then she smiled. "I need to take Holly home then take care of your chores at the plantation." He turned to Whit. "Thank you for your diligence. Are these the same men you overheard the other night?"

"They are. I should still be able to give you a hand for a few hours today, if you're still interested in hiring me."

"When you can, come in. I will be there. It is going to take me a bit to take Miss Landers home."

Whit smiled. "Thank you again for the job."

"You are welcome. And thank you for your help today." Bryce looked back at the three bandits. "I appreciate it."

"My pleasure."

"All right," Chad interrupted, "enough of the gushy stuff. Time is a'wasting. I have plans with a pretty young lady and I don't want to keep her waiting." Chad smiled.

Bryce laughed. "Priorities, little brother. Priorities."

"You betcha. Come on, guys." Chad pointed his rifle at them and encouraged the men to start walking toward town. Whit climbed back up on his horse and rode beside Chad.

Holly's wide eyes darted between him and the other men. "Did you set this up? You told the men that there were people coming. I thought you were just posturing. But you knew?"

"No, I did not set it up, but I knew Mr. Butterfield would be coming along fairly soon to meet me at the plantation. And I knew Chadwick had planned an early afternoon visit with a certain young lady in town. I am thankful they arrived when they did."

"You and me both. I'm still shaking."

"I know, honey. I am sorry you had to hear such dreadful things. I would never have let them take you."

"I know, but there were three of them and…" The floodgates opened and Holly crumpled into his arms. "Oh, Bryce, I was so scared."

"I know. It is all right now. The Lord protected us." Bryce silently prayed his thanksgiving to the Lord for their protection. He wrapped her in his arms and held her until she calmed.

Holly eased out of his embrace. "Thank you. I'm okay now."

"We have had quite a day, haven't we? First your memory of falling into a well and then this. I am glad those bandits were caught. Now I will not be so nervous with you driving back and forth from the plantation to the city."

Holly rubbed her arms and tried to concentrate on their surroundings rather than on the unsettled feelings that had emerged since the bandits had appeared. It brought back the night Bryce had been shot and the fear she'd felt of being buried deep in the earth. She could almost picture it. The taste of the dirt and the smell of the damp stale air swirled around in her memory.

"Holly?" Bryce's voice penetrated her thoughts. She wanted to answer him but she couldn't speak, not yet.

"Holly?" His voice quivered.

Holly pointed her index finger toward heaven. *Give me a moment, please,* she silently pleaded.

Bryce nodded and took the reins. He snapped them lightly and the buggy eased forward. He kept a slow pace.

Holly started to count. One. She took a breath, eased it out. Two. She repeated the process. Three. Her chest heaved slightly then relaxed. "I'm recalling more of the incident when I was a little girl, very young. I felt alone and trapped. I'm fairly certain I fell down a well of some sort."

Bryce reached over and took her hand. "What else do you remember?"

"They are more feelings than actual memories. I can almost taste the dirt. That's it. The smell of the yard when we walked out of the house… There was something similar in that backyard that smelled like the well I was in."

Bryce caressed the top of her hand with his thumb. He didn't speak. She sensed he was waiting on her, on the memories. "I was cold, damp, even wet. It was like I was sitting in a puddle. Which makes sense if it was an old well."

He nodded and waited. Her love for him grew even more. "You're incredible, do you know that?"

He winked. "Let the memories flow."

"I think the fear of the bandits, combined with the earlier memories, are helping them come to the surface. I remember something like a bucket being lowered to me. But it wasn't a bucket. It was larger. Darker. As it came toward me it blocked all the light. I started to scream, I think. I'm not sure. It's all so confusing." .

"You are doing fine, Holly." He gave a light squeeze to her hand.

She glanced over at his honey-brown eyes. Warmth spread through her heart to every part of her body. "I love you."

"I love you, too." He smiled. "Do you think the bucket was a person coming down the well to help you?"

"It must have been. I was so scared, terrified. Wait…" Gooseflesh rose on her skin. "I know the voice. It was my dad, Emmett Landers. He rescued me. He called my name. He said, 'Holly, pumpkin, it's Daddy. I'm here to rescue you.' It wasn't John Graham. It was Emmett. I must have seen him when I was little. Perhaps when he came to reclaim Mother and me. But why would I have been in a well? And where was my father?" Then another image appeared. "I was brought out of the pit, or the well, in Emmett's arms, but I reached for John. Then I heard Emmett say to me, 'I'm your daddy, Holly, but John is your father.' He kissed me and handed me over to John. Both my fathers were there. They worked together to save me."

Bryce smiled. "Amazing! Not only in that moment, but in all aspects of your life they have been working together.

Granted, Emmett went back to Tennessee but he never stopped loving and caring for you. He did just as he said. He gave you up for your sake. He recognized John as the man given the task to raise you, being your father."

"That has to be why I stopped calling John 'Daddy.' The day of Mother's funeral when I met Emmett, my body reacted. It's as if I knew who he was without knowing."

"You recognized his voice and probably him, but could not grasp how you knew him. You just reacted."

The memory resurfaced in full color. She saw herself wandering off, going somewhere she wasn't supposed to and falling into an old well shaft. She had no idea how long she had been down in that hole, but it had been awhile. "I wonder where this happened."

"I am sure your father will remember."

"More than likely. I wonder why we never talked about it."

Bryce leveled his gaze at hers. "And bring up the fact that you had another father?"

"Ah," Holly moaned. "I must have decided not to call John 'Daddy' because I had another daddy who saved me. But there was a peace being in John's arms, as well. I've always found comfort in my father's loving arms."

They pulled up in front of the Graham plantation house but neither got out of the buggy. Bryce turned and took her hands in his.

"The conversation he and you had the day after you were shot?"

"You heard?"

"Yes. So, you have John Graham's blessings to marry me."

Bryce chuckled. "Yes, I do. However, I have not asked you to marry me, yet." He wiggled his eyebrows.

Holly giggled. "True, but I also have not accepted because you have not asked. And who is to say whether or not I will accept. After all, you still haven't kissed me and…"

Bryce pulled her into an embrace. His lips were a fraction of an inch from hers. He shifted his head and leaned toward her ear. "I will kiss you when the time is right. Besides, you know who is holding that kiss up. It isn't me, is it?" he whispered.

A shiver sizzled down her spine. "But I want to kiss you."

"And you shall, when you are ready. How is that harness on your heart, now that you have recovered this memory?" He leaned away from her but fixed his gaze.

They were silently speaking with one another. She examined her heart. The tightness was disappearing little by little. Frustrated, she pulled away. "It's still there."

He caressed her shoulders. "But is it smaller than this morning?"

"Yes, but don't you think kissing me might dissolve it altogether?" Holly crossed her arms and exhaled.

"Possibly. Let us deal with this new memory. Then we can discuss your commitment to me or not."

He turned to face her and grasped her hands in his. "Honey, no doubts can be present when we commit to one another, not even a slight one. There will come days when we question why we would want to marry one another. It is all a part of growing in love. I want us to have a firm foundation to build our marriage on. Please bear with me about this kiss. We will both know when the time is right. My passion is strong for you, and I would like nothing more than to sweep you in my arms and kiss you. But my commitment to you the night of your mother's funeral is more important. I gave you my word. You need to know without a doubt for our future that I will keep my word even when I want something so very much. You are the one I will commit my life to. And while kissing you would be easy, we cannot afford to."

Holly glanced down at their hands intertwined together. "Thank you for being a man of your word and not giving in to my foolish desires."

"Honey, there is nothing foolish about your desire. I am rather happy that you have it, excited really." He beamed. "However, as I mentioned, there is more at stake, and we have to do this right. You are certainly less vulnerable than the night of your mother's funeral but…"

"I haven't completely rid myself of the fear," she said, finishing his thought. "I'm still dealing with anger and frustration about my past and the betrayal I felt from my mom. Do you think I will ever be completely free of those emotions?"

"I believe so. I also believe they will come up again from time to time in the future. Not being able to discuss all of this with your mother leaves doubt and confusion in your mind that will never be totally resolved. However, you shall eventually be free from its chains. Just look at the day you have had today."

"Yes, but what if I can never be rid of this wall in my heart?"

Bryce pulled her into an embrace. "You will, honey. I know it. I cannot explain it, but I know it is coming. We can manage these obstacles. I promise."

Holly leaned into his shoulder and relaxed. Her heart beat wildly in her chest. She loved him so much. And when she was in his arms everything else around her vanished. She closed her eyes and absorbed his love, his strength, his peace and the confidence that everything, absolutely everything, would work out. "Oh, Bryce, I love you."

"I love you, too." He kissed the top of her head. She smiled. He was kissing her, just not on her lips.

"When I'm in your arms like this, I don't feel the resistance. Does that count?"

He tilted her face to meet his. "Yes." He closed his eyes and pushed away from her. She felt the sudden coolness between them. "Soon, my love. We shall be kissing very soon."

"Cannot be soon enough," she mumbled and got down from the buggy.

Bryce strained every muscle in his body not to give in to his desires for Holly. Perhaps later tonight he might be able to kiss her. If he didn't soon, they'd be sending him off to the asylum. *Dear God, give me strength. I don't know if I can hold out much longer.*

Bryce secured the buggy and hopped down to join Holly. "Shall we go see if your father is free?"

Holly giggled. "He is. He's in the window. I imagine he saw us carrying on."

Bryce groaned. He held out his arm for her.

"Relax, we didn't even kiss. Not for a lack of trying on my part."

The touch of her hand in the crook of his elbow calmed him. "I am aware of that. You are temptation with a capital *T,* I will have you know."

"Good."

Bryce shook his head from side to side. "It shall be an interesting marriage."

"If you ever ask me," she teased.

"Let us not bring that discussion up again right now. We have bigger concerns."

Holly grew somber. "Yes. Yes, we do." They walked into the house and headed straight for her father's study.

"Good afternoon, Mr. Graham." Bryce extended his hand.

John Graham received it and gave a firm handshake. "Mr. Jarvis." He leaned over and kissed his daughter on the cheek. "Hello, daughter."

"Hello, Father."

John motioned for them to sit. Bryce took the lead. "Holly had a memory surface this morning and she would like to discuss it with you."

John sat straight and gripped the arms of his chair. "What memory, sweetheart?"

"Did I fall down a well when I was really young?"

John paled. "Yes. Yes, you did."

"Was my father Emmett Landers there? Did he come down inside the well and carry me out?"

"Yes."

"And were you there, as well, helping us out?"

"Yes. I held the rope and ran it through a pulley."

"How did it happen?" Holly leaned forward.

"You were always an inquisitive child and one day you wandered off. Your father Emmett had come back with the legal papers. The four of us went to visit with his mother and your mother's mother. The two women weren't exactly on speaking terms with one another.... As best we could figure it at the time, you wandered outside to the backyard and fell through an old boarded-up well where the wood had rotted out. Fortunately your father knew how to track and found you rather quickly. It did take some time to rig the pulleys and rope to rescue you. But apart from that, nothing else happened."

"Actually, something did. I believe when Emmett rescued me, to calm me he said he was my daddy. When we surfaced he told me you were my father. I believe that is why I stopped calling you 'Daddy.'"

John leaned back in his seat and pondered the new revelation. Slowly his head began to nod. "You are probably right. It was around that time that you stopped."

Holly leaned back in her chair. Bryce watched the two of them.

"What did he say, exactly?" John asked.

"He said, 'Holly, pumpkin, it's Daddy. I'm here to rescue you.' After we got out of the well and I reached for you he said, 'I'm your daddy, Holly, but John is your father.'"

"That sounds like Emmett. We had been discussing how much contact he should have with you once he left the area. He and his mother wanted you to visit over the summer months. Your grandmothers argued about it. Your mother cried. She couldn't picture you being gone from her sight for so long. That's when Emmett decided he would have no contact with you until you knew the truth. He's an honorable man. He's never gone back on his word. I was too afraid of you knowing about him when you were vulnerable. I am the one at fault, not your mother or father. Blame me for the past, Holly."

Gentle tears slipped from the corners of Holly's eyes. Bryce swallowed the lump forming in his own throat. Holly looked at her father, her eyes glistening. "I understand, Father, and I forgive you. I forgive you with all of my heart for everything."

Bryce reached over and grasped her hand, giving it a gentle squeeze. Holly's gaze pierced his. Her eyes sparkled with unshed tears, but there was something more. They smiled with joy. In that very moment of forgiveness she found the release she longed for. Now he couldn't wait to kiss her.

Chapter 15

Bryce had departed several days earlier with the lingering whisper, "I shall return as soon as possible." She knew he would be busy for the next two days. She hoped she'd see him tonight.

"What are you working on?" Tiffany asked.

"Some Irish lace. Would you like to try to learn again?"

Tiffany plopped down on Holly's bed. "No, I've tried too many times. It's not for me. What are you going to make?"

"Some Christmas presents for my other sisters. I was thinking in terms of some lace purses."

"Christmas? That's a few months away."

"True, but they live in Tennessee. Who knows how long it will take a package to arrive? I'll also make a purse for my stepmother."

Tiffany scrunched up her nose. "Isn't it odd to call someone stepmother?"

"Yes and no. It's odd because I've never known her until recently. On the other hand, it is how I came to know her, so she is who she is."

"I suppose." Tiffany looked down at the floor then up at Holly again. Holly put down her lacework and braced for something serious. "You still haven't kissed Bryce yet, have you?"

Holly raised her right eyebrow.

"I saw you the other day in the buggy. He held you close but you and he never kissed. How is that possible?"

"It took a great deal of self-control." More on his part than her own.

"Why wait? I mean, you're planning on marrying him, aren't you?"

"We're talking about the possibility. Nothing formal has been offered or asked yet."

"I don't understand why kissing is such a big deal."

"For personal reasons I cannot explain right now."

"What reasons? What would keep you from kissing the man you love? And you do love Bryce. You cannot deny it."

Holly paused. "Yes, I do love Bryce." Should she explain? She glanced at her sister's questioning eyes. Perhaps Tiff could learn from her and Bryce. "I'll tell you, but this will be our secret. Not because it is anything bad— just personal."

Tiffany leaned in closer.

"The night of Mother's funeral Bryce and I were in the barn. He was helping me sort out what I'd just learned about my parentage. I found myself very attracted to Bryce and leaned in to kiss him. He pulled away, not because he didn't want to kiss me but because he felt I was vulnerable. He was right. That kiss, while I imagine it would have been pleasant enough, would have been an emotional response. I would have kissed him because I'd needed compassion, not because of my great love for him. Does this make sense?"

"Kinda. But why aren't you kissing him now?"

Holly sighed. "Because Bryce, being a man of his word, promised he would not kiss me until all the pain, hurt, confused emotions and doubt were gone from my heart."

"You're still hurting?"

"Yes, but not in the same way. The other day, the one in which you saw us embracing in the buggy, I was freed from the final pain in my heart. Unfortunately, Bryce hasn't been able to come by since that day so we still haven't kissed." Holly groaned.

Tiffany laughed. "Ya'll are in love then?"

"Yes." Holly chuckled along with her sister.

"Holly?" The running footfalls of her brother Riley came toward them. "Papa says you need to come quick."

Holly and Tiffany jumped up and met Riley at the doorway. "What's the matter?"

"Don't know, just have to come quick."

Holly pushed past her brother and ran down the stairs. "Where's Father?"

"In the back garden." Holly ran to the back of the house and out the doors leading to the veranda. Her gaze darted side to side searching for her father. "Father, where are you? What's the matter?"

He eased up from his crouched position, brushing off his knees. "What's the matter, Holly?"

"Riley said you wanted me to come quickly... I didn't see you... I panicked."

He stood to his full height. "I did ask Riley to fetch you, but I asked him to be quick about it because he was lollygagging."

"Oh, sorry." Riley ran off toward the barn.

Tiffany waved off the commotion and went back inside. "What did you need to see me about, Father?"

"Bryce sent a message that he'll be coming around five to pick you up for dinner and the theater tonight. He'd like you to dress in evening attire." John grinned. Gone was any misguided resentment toward Bryce.

Holly smiled. She had the perfect outfit. Her emerald-green dress with no sleeves. Mindful of propriety, she would wear a shawl made of Irish lace to cover her arms and shoulders. "Thank you, Father. I need to get ready."

He smiled. "Have fun tonight, Holly."

"Thanks, Daddy." She winked.

John's smile brightened.

Bryce straightened his tie and polished the top of each boot with a swipe across the back of his trouser legs. His tie adjusted, he knocked on the front door.

Calvin opened the door and smiled. "Evening, Bryce."

"Good evening, Calvin."

"She's all fancied up. Where ya takin' her?"

"To a restaurant and a theater show."

"Treat her right. I know how to shoot, ya know."

Bryce held back his laughter. A seven-year-old protecting his sister's honor was not something to mess with. Riley was next in line with his arms crossed, scanning him from head to toe and back again. "Good evening, Riley."

"Evenin', Bryce. You be careful taking her home tonight."

"Yes, sir. You do know we caught the bandits?"

"Yes, but there might be others trying their hand at easy money."

"I will be careful." Daniel and Tiffany smiled. Tiffany seemed downright giddy.

Holly appeared at the top of the stairway and paused.

His breath caught. His mouth slackened as he took in the vision of regal beauty. She wore a long dress of emerald green that hung delicately off the edge of her soft, creamy white shoulders. White Irish lace bordered the squared neckline. A thin gold chain held an excellently cut emerald, matched by a set of earrings, highlighting the green of her eyes. Her lovely red hair was pulled tightly back and up, with a few wavy strands breaking free around her face. "You take my breath away, Holly. You are the most beautiful woman I've ever seen."

Holly glided down the stairs as if walking on air. This side of Holly was new to him. "You are stunning."

"You are rather dapper yourself," she said with a wink.

He held out his arm. "Shall we?" The ring in his pocket seemed to be on fire. He couldn't wait to put it on her finger. *Lord, help me wait until the right moment.*

"With pleasure, Mr. Jarvis." She placed her hand in the crook of his elbow and he captured her hand with his own.

John Graham cleared his throat. Bryce turned to see him leaning against the door casing to his office. "Yes, sir?"

"Best wishes on your evening together."

"Thank you, sir."

"Good night, Daddy."

John smiled. Bryce squeezed her hand and thanked the Lord for the healing that had come into Holly's life. Outside, Ryan sat perched above the front wheel, on the landau's driver's bench. The carriage's leather top was up. "Ryan has agreed to be our driver tonight so you can have my undivided attention."

"I'm honored."

"Honey, I must admit, I would rather forgo dinner and the show and spend the evening together alone. However, having the most enchanting woman in all of Savannah, possibly all of Georgia, on my arm at dinner and the theater will make me the envy of every man in town."

Holly gave a bashful look toward the ground. "I'm glad you like the dress."

"You never cease to amaze me, Holly." He helped her step up into the carriage.

Once they were inside, Ryan drove the carriage toward the city.

"Let me look at you. You're magnificent, simply stunning. You took my breath away when I saw you on top of the stairs. I love you, Holly."

"I love you, too, Bryce. And there is nothing stopping me from loving you completely. The hard place in my heart is gone."

"I'm so happy. And I'm so happy I waited to do this in the way that such a precious woman deserves." Bryce slid off the seat and knelt in front of her. "Holly Elizabeth Landers, you are the most intriguing woman I know. I love you with all my heart and I would love the honor of becoming your husband, if you will have me. Will you marry me?"

"Only if you kiss me."

Bryce moaned but regained his seat next to Holly and wrapped her in his arms. With all the tenderness he could muster he captured her lips with his. His pulse quickened. The world faded away. The kiss deepened. He was hers forever and always.

Holly's eyes remained closed for a moment after Bryce pulled away. Slowly she blinked her eyes open. She looked into his honey-brown depths and caressed his cheek with her thumb. "Yes, I will marry you, Bryce. You are my closest friend, the one person I could share all my deepest secrets with. You are my love and my passion is for you and only you."

Bryce's smile deepened. He reached into his pocket. "I hope this ring will fit. I had Tiffany sneak me one of your rings so I could have the jeweler size it."

"Tiffany knew before I did?"

Bryce chuckled. "It only seemed fitting since she knew two years ago my intentions to court you."

Holly slapped him on the shoulder.

"Ow! What was that for?"

"From now on you come to me first."

He rubbed his arm. "Of course."

"Bryce, I love you. Thank you for being patient with me, for helping me through the past several months. I don't think I could have made it without you."

"You could have because you are a strong woman. However, I am glad to have been there to help you through, to pray you through, to be the man you needed during this difficult time. I love you, Holly."

"I love you, too." She leaned in and he leaned toward her. Their lips touched again, this time with gentle passion. When they separated, she asked, "So, when did you want to get married?"

"It depends on you. I am planning a two-month honeymoon—a sea voyage to Italy, nearly two weeks there, first stop Venice, of course. Then a cruise home. Does that sound acceptable to you?"

"Did you say Venice?" Holly's heart couldn't beat any faster.

"Yes."

"How soon can we go? Wait, we haven't even courted yet."

Bryce chuckled. "No, I suppose that is true. Unofficially, wouldn't you agree that we have been courting all our lives, getting to know one another? We could marry quickly but we wouldn't be home for Christmas. Would that suit you?"

"For Venice, with you? Yes! I'm comfortable leaving the family behind. Just how much profit did you make on the sale of the house?"

"Enough." He smiled.

"Can I kiss you again? I cannot believe we waited so long."

"We were not waiting, you were healing, Holly. There is a difference."

"I know and I appreciate your patience with me. Still, I'd like another kiss, if you don't mind?"

"Kissing you, love, will never be a problem."

Holly eased into Bryce's arms. Her heart was at peace. Her mother's and fathers' decisions seemed a distant hurt from the past. Today she was beginning her life as the future Mrs. Bryce Jarvis and, oddly enough, the name change seemed a perfect fit.

* * * * *

SPECIAL EXCERPT FROM

Love Inspired

He was her high school crush, and now he's a single father of twins. Allison True just got a second chance at love.

Read on for a sneak preview of
STORYBOOK ROMANCE by Lissa Manley,
the exciting fifth book in
THE HEART OF MAIN STREET series,
available October 2013.

Something clunked from the back of the bookstore, drawing Allison True's ever-vigilant attention. Her ears perking up, she rounded the end of the front counter. Another clunk sounded, and then another. Allison decided the noise was coming from the Kids' Korner, so she picked up the pace and veered toward the back right part of the store, creasing her brow.

She arrived in the area set up for kids. Her gaze zeroed in on a dark-haired toddler dressed in jeans and a red shirt, slowly yet methodically yanking books off a shelf, one after the other. Each book fell to the floor with a heavy clunk, and in between each sound, the little guy laughed, clearly enjoying the sound of his relatively harmless yet messy play.

Allison rushed over, noting there was no adult in sight. "Hey, there, bud," she said. "Whatcha doing?"

He turned big brown eyes fringed with long, dark eyelashes toward her. He looked vaguely familiar even though she was certain she'd never met this little boy.

"Fun!" A chubby hand sent another book crashing to the floor. He giggled and stomped his feet on the floor in a little happy dance. "See?"

Carefully she reached out and stilled his marauding hands. "Whoa, there, little guy." She gently pulled him away. "The books are supposed to stay on the shelf." Holding on to him, she cast her gaze about the enclosed area set aside for kids, but her view was limited by the tall bookshelves lined up from the edge of the Kids' Korner to the front of the store. "Are you here with your mommy or daddy?"

The boy tugged. "Daddy!" he squealed.

"Nicky!" a deep masculine voice replied behind her. "Oh, man. Looks like you've been making a mess."

A nebulous sense of familiarity swept through her at the sound of that voice. Not breathing, still holding the boy's hand, Allison slowly turned around. Her whole body froze and her heart gave a little spasm then fell to her toes as she looked into deep brown eyes that matched Nicky's.

Sam Franklin. The only man Allison had ever loved.

Pick up STORYBOOK ROMANCE
in October 2013 wherever Love Inspired® Books are sold.

REQUEST YOUR FREE BOOKS!

2 FREE CHRISTIAN NOVELS
PLUS 2
FREE
MYSTERY GIFTS

HEARTSONG
PRESENTS

YES! Please send me 2 Free Heartsong Presents novels and my 2 FREE mystery gifts (gifts are worth about $10). After receiving them, if I don't wish to receive any more books I can return the shipping statement marked "cancel." If I don't cancel, I will receive 4 brand-new novels every month and be billed just $4.24 per book in the U.S. and $5.24 per book in Canada. That's a savings of at least 20% off the cover price. It's quite a bargain! Shipping and handling is just 50¢ per book in the U.S. and 75¢ per book in Canada.* I understand that accepting the 2 free books and gifts places me under no obligation to buy anything. I can always return a shipment and cancel at any time. Even if I never buy another book, the two free books and gifts are mine to keep forever.

159/359 HDN FVYK

Name _____ (PLEASE PRINT) _____

Address _____ Apt. # _____

City _____ State _____ Zip _____

Signature (if under 18, a parent or guardian must sign)

Mail to the **Harlequin® Reader Service:**
IN U.S.A.: P.O. Box 1867, Buffalo, NY 14240-1867

* Terms and prices subject to change without notice. Prices do not include applicable taxes. Sales tax applicable in N.Y. This offer is limited to one order per household. Not valid for current subscribers to Heartsong Presents books. All orders subject to credit approval. Credit or debit balances in a customer's account(s) may be offset by any other outstanding balance owed by or to the customer. Please allow 4 to 6 weeks for delivery. Offer available while quantities last. Offer valid only in the U.S.

Your Privacy—The Harlequin® Reader Service is committed to protecting your privacy. Our Privacy Policy is available online at www.ReaderService.com or upon request from the Harlequin Reader Service.
We make a portion of our mailing list available to reputable third parties that offer products we believe may interest you. If you prefer that we not exchange your name with third parties, or if you wish to clarify or modify your communication preferences, please visit us at www.ReaderService.com/consumerschoice or write to us at Harlequin Reader Service Preference Service, P.O. Box 9062, Buffalo, NY 14269. Include your complete name and address.

HEARTSONG
PRESENTS

Look out for 4 new
Heartsong Presents books next month!

**Every month 4 inspiring faith-filled
romances will be available in stores.**

These contemporary and historical Christian
romances emphasize God's role in every
relationship and reinforce the importance of
faith, hope and love.

Eve Pickering knows what it's like to be judged because of your past. So she's not about to leave the orphaned boy she's befriended alone and unprotected in this unfamiliar Texas town. And if Chance Dawson's offer of shelter is the only way she can look after Leo, Eve will turn it into a warm, welcoming home for the holidays. No matter how temporary it may be—or how much she's really longing to stay for good....

Chance came all the way from the big city to make it on his own in spite of his secret...and his overbearing rich family. But Eve's bravery and caring is giving him a confidence he never expected— and a new direction for his dream. And with a little Christmas luck, he'll dare to win her heart as well as her trust—and make their family one for a lifetime.

Texas Grooms

A Family for Christmas

by

WINNIE GRIGGS

Available October 2013 wherever
Love Inspired Historical books are sold.

LIH82983

Love Inspired SUSPENSE

RIVETING INSPIRATIONAL ROMANCE

FALL FROM GRACE by **MARTA PERRY**

Teacher Sara Esch helps widower Caleb King comfort his daughter who witnessed a crime. But then Sara gets too close to the truth and Caleb must risk it all for the woman who's taught him to love again.

DANGEROUS HOMECOMING by **DIANE BURKE**

Katie Lapp needs her childhood friend Joshua Miller more than ever when someone threatens her late husband's farm. Katie wants it settled the Amish way...but not everyone can be trusted. Can Joshua protect her...even if it endangers his heart?

RETURN TO WILLOW TRACE by **KIT WILKINSON**

Lydia Stoltz wants to avoid the man who courted her years ago. But a series of accidents startles their Plain community...and leads her straight to Joseph Yoder. At every turn, it seems their shared past holds the key to their future.

DANGER IN AMISH COUNTRY,

a 3-in-1 anthology including novellas by
MARTA PERRY, DIANE BURKE and
KIT WILKINSON

*Available October 2013 wherever
Love Inspired Suspense books are sold.*

Find us on Facebook at
www.Facebook.com/LoveInspiredBooks

LIS44558R

Allison True knows that in real life, romances end in heartache. She learned that the hard way in high school, when handsome Sam Franklin completely ignored her existence. Back in Bygones, Allison is older now, and wiser. Her only focus is keeping her new bookstore afloat, and her heart safe from Sam.

Before he was a single dad juggling rambunctious twins, Sam had a secret thing for Allison. Now a beautiful young woman has replaced the bookish girl in braids and glasses, and Sam must work twice as hard to keep his feelings in check. He swore off love after his ex shattered his heart and his faith. But Allison seems to know the secret to repairing both....

The Cowboy's Christmas Courtship
by Brenda Minton

Available October 2013
wherever Love Inspired books are sold.

LI87843

Love the Love Inspired book you just read?

Your opinion matters.

Review this book on your favorite book site, review site, blog or your own social media properties and share your opinion with other readers!

Be sure to connect with us at:
Harlequin.com/Newsletters
Twitter.com/LoveInspiredBks
Facebook.com/LoveInspiredBooks